No One Must Know

EVA WISEMAN

Tundra Books

Published in Canada by Tundra Books,
75 Sherbourne Street, Toronto, Ontario M5A 2P9

Published in the United States by Tundra Books of Northern
New York, P.O. Box 1030, Plattsburgh, New York 12901

Library of Congress Control Number: 2004106595

National Library of Canada Cataloguing in Publication

Wiseman, Eva, 1947-
No one must know / Eva Wiseman.

ISBN 978-0-88776-680-0

1. Jews – Persecutions – Juvenile fiction.   2. Hungarian
Canadians – Juvenile fiction.   I. Title.

ps8595.i814n6 2004   jc813'.54   c2004-902771-9

We acknowledge the financial support of the Government of
Canada through the Book Publishing Industry Development
Program (BPIDP) and that of the Ontario Media Development
Corporation's Ontario Book Initiative. We further acknowledge
the support of the Canada Council for the Arts and the
Ontario Arts Council for our publishing program.

Design: Terri Nimmo
Printed and bound in Canada

This book is printed on acid-free paper that is 100% recycled,
ancient-forest friendly (40% post-consumer recycled).

2 3 4 5 6   12 11 10 09 08

For my parents and my husband

Acknowledgments

I want to thank my family for their help and their belief in me. I would like to acknowledge the assistance of the Manitoba Arts Council and the Canada Council for the Arts. John Matthews and Ben and Yolanda Arroz taught me all I know about five-pin bowling, and Sally Corby shared her enthusiasm for the Girl Guides. Father Mike Koryluk and Monsignor Norman J. Chartrand patiently answered my questions. As always, my editors, Kathy Lowinger and Janice Weaver, inspired me to do my best.

And then there were the seven courageous individuals in Winnipeg, Toronto, and Budapest who shared their secrets with me. I will be forever grateful for the trust they placed in me. I just hope I did justice to their stories.

Our deeds still travel with us from afar,
And what we have been makes us what we are.

– George Eliot, *Middlemarch*

Chapter 1

✻✻✻✻✻✻✻✻✻✻✻✻✻✻✻✻✻✻✻✻✻✻✻✻✻✻✻✻

"**M**ove over!" I cried. "You're blocking my sun."

"Lazybones!" Molly said as she plopped herself down on a towel spread out next to mine on the sand. "You should go for a swim. The water is perfect, and you're getting burned."

"My mother says that too much sun will give you freckles," Jean said from my other side.

"I'm not going to worry about *that*! I just want a tan for the first day of school."

My eyes swept across the beach full of sun worshippers, prone bodies of every shape and size baking on the golden sand. A few steps away the surface of the lake gleamed azure, and in the distance the white sails of sailboats fluttered in the gentle breeze.

"Can you rub oil on my back?" Jean asked.

"Sure. Pull down your straps." As usual, she was wearing a one-piece bathing suit. I applied gobs of lotion to her shoulder blades.

"It's so nice here," she said. "I can hardly believe school is only two weeks away."

"Don't even mention it," Molly said. "I want this summer to go on forever." She stretched her skinny arms wide. "I'm so hot! I don't know how you can stand lying in the sun for so long." She stood up. "Can either of you lend me a dime? I want to buy an ice-cream cone."

"I don't have a penny," Jean mumbled. "I spent all of my baby-sitting money on nylons."

"I'm broke too," I said, "but let me talk to Mom and Dad. Maybe they'll give me an advance on my allowance. If we're lucky, they might even treat us."

I held out my hand and Molly pulled me up. After I'd smoothed down the pink gingham skirt of my new two-piece bathing suit, I was ready to go. "You coming with us, Jean?"

"No," she said with her eyes closed. She patted her stomach. "Do I look like I need ice cream? I'll stay here and work on my freckles."

My parents were just a few feet away, sitting on a

bench under a tree at the edge of the sand. Dad wore a striped bathing suit, but Mom was buttoned up in a long-sleeved summer dress even though it was a hot day. She had her bad leg, in its ugly orthopedic shoe, stuck out in front of her, her cane by her side. As soon as she saw us, she straightened up.

"What's up?" Dad asked. He moved closer to Mom to make room for us on the bench.

"You look a little burnt, darling," Mom said to me. "You too, Molly. Stay out of the sun. I promised your mother we'd take good care of you."

"Thank you for inviting me to come to the beach with you, Mrs. Gal," Molly said.

"Our pleasure." Mom smiled. "It's so lovely here. It reminds me of Lake Balaton, in the old country. We used to spend our summers there before the war," she said in a wistful tone. Then she shook her head, as if to chase away the memories. "Are you two having fun?" she asked.

"We want to buy ice-cream cones, but we don't –"

"Have enough money!" Mom completed my sentence. "What else is new?"

Dad reached into his pocket and pulled out a dollar bill. "This should cover it. Alexandra, could you bring me back a vanilla cone, one scoop only?"

"I sure will! Thanks, Dad. What about you, Mom?"

"Nothing for me, dear. Go and enjoy yourselves."

"Your parents are such nice people," Molly said as we clomped through the sand.

"I can lend them to you if you'd like! Sometimes they make me feel like a prisoner."

She laughed. "I know what you mean. My parents treat me like a four-year-old."

We joined a long line in front of the snack bar. The customers were in a festive mood. A couple in front of us were necking, oblivious to the world. Three young boys behind us were throwing a football around wildly. Behind them stood a tall blond boy about our age.

"He is *so* cute!" I whispered to Molly. "Do you know who he is?"

"He *is* adorable," she said. "But I haven't seen him before. He must be new at the beach."

Finally, it was our turn. Molly bought a strawberry milkshake while I got my favorite – a sugar cone with two scoops of chocolate ice cream – and Dad's single scoop of vanilla. I was balancing Dad's ice cream in my left hand and licking the chocolate cone in my right when I heard Molly cry out.

"Alex! Look out!"

As I glanced up, my breath caught in my throat – a football was flying in my direction at full speed! Everything happened so fast that I didn't have time to dodge the ball or even to drop the ice-cream cones and put my hands in front of my face. I froze in my tracks, waiting for the ball to smash into me. Suddenly the blond boy dived forward, stretched his arms high, and struck the ball with his fists, pushing it off its collision course with me.

I stared at him with my mouth half open and my hands gripping the wobbly ice-cream cones, too stunned even to thank him. The boys, meanwhile, grabbed their football and ran away without a word.

"Stupid kids," the blond boy said with a shy smile. "You could have been badly hurt."

"Next," said the soda jerk in a bored voice. The blond boy stepped up to the window and placed his order.

"Ask his name," Molly whispered.

"I can't!"

"Then tell him your name. Introduce yourself."

"I don't have the nerve."

While I waited in an agony of indecision, the soda jerk gave the blond boy a bag of chips and a bottle of Coke. He paid for his purchases and, with a smile over his shoulder, left before I said a single word.

"We have to follow him," Molly cried, pulling me after her, "or we'll never see him again!"

We spotted him a few feet ahead of us, picking his way through the carpet of bodies. Just as we were gaining on him, he turned on his heel and crossed the imaginary line that divided the beach into two equal halves. To the left of this line was the Jewish section, to the right our section. We never crossed this line to sit on the Jewish side, and the Jews never crossed over to our side.

"He's from Jew beach!" Molly said, coming to such a sudden stop that I bumped into her. We just stood there, staring after him until he disappeared into the throng of bodies on the sand. We couldn't think what else to do but turn back and take Dad's melting ice cream to him.

For the last two weekends of the summer, I searched and searched for the boy with the blond hair each time we drove out to the lake. I didn't see him again. Whenever I arrived at the imaginary line that separated the Jews' beach from ours, I always stopped.

Chapter 2

꙳꙳꙳꙳꙳꙳꙳꙳꙳꙳꙳꙳꙳꙳꙳꙳꙳꙳꙳꙳꙳꙳꙳꙳꙳꙳꙳꙳

The blue uniform fitted me to perfection. I tightened the wide leather belt around my waist, straightened the light blue tie around my neck, and yanked down my beret until it rested at a raffish angle above my right eye. Then I pulled the thin gold cross I always wore around my neck from the folds of the blue kerchief. One of my knee-highs was sagging, so I crouched down and yanked it up. As I was straightening up, I caught a glimpse of myself in the full-length mirror hanging on the wall by my bed. A stranger with my features was staring back at me. With her crisp uniform, the girl in the mirror seemed out of place in my crowded bedroom with its white-and-gold furniture and canopied bed. A ruffled pink bedspread covered the bed and a pink carpet lay on the hardwood floor. On the wall above the dresser hung a poster of Elvis, cute as ever in his army uniform. The poster, which I'd bought with my baby-sitting money, was surrounded by vines laden with pink rose-buds, the design on the wallpaper. I pirouetted in front of the mirror with a satisfied sigh – the uniformed girl it reflected seemed so much older and more sophisticated than my usual self.

"Alexandra, breakfast is ready. Hurry up!" Mom called from downstairs.

I tore myself away from the mirror and slid down the banister. With Dad busy with his patients at his Saturday morning clinic in his office down the street and Mom occupied in the kitchen, I knew there was nobody around to warn me that I would break my neck.

As I entered the kitchen, my eyes fell on a thick book lying open on the table beside a cup of coffee and an ashtray overflowing with cigarette butts. Mom was at the stove with her back to me. As always, she was fashion-ably dressed, with not a strand of her curly hair out of place. The long sleeves of her dress were pushed up to her elbows, revealing a white scar on the underside of one arm, above her wrist. She was humming a bright Hungarian tune. She leaned heavily on her cane as she flipped an egg in the frying pan. The aromas wafting from the pan made my mouth water.

I stopped in the doorway and struck a pose like a fashion model – arms akimbo and hips thrusting forward. "Good morning!" I said.

"Eggs for breakfast," she replied without turning around. She reached up with her right hand, took a plate from the cupboard above the stove, and put it on the counter. She ladled a generous helping of eggs onto the plate before picking it up again and swiveling around to face me. "I hope you'll eat . . ." Her voice died out as she caught sight of me in the doorway, and she dropped the plate onto the countertop with a clank, almost spilling its contents. She didn't say a word, just stared at me white-faced, her mouth a wide O.

"What's the matter?" I asked. "Don't you like my uniform?"

"I do, I do, darling," she said slowly, her accent heavy in my ears. "Your uniform is lovely. It's just that it reminded me of something else. Back home, during the war . . ."

Once again her voice trailed off. My ears perked up, however, for she rarely talked about her life during the war. All I knew was that my parents had arrived in Canada shortly after its end, before I was born, and that they had named me after my grandmother.

Mom talked all the time about how difficult everything had been in the beginning. She was proud that Dad had learned English and had passed his Canadian medical exams with ease. "That's because your father is a wonderful doctor," she often said. But if I asked her to tell me why they left Europe, she clammed up. I had learned a long time ago that my parents' experiences during and just after the war were a closed book, a book I was never allowed to read.

Once, when I was still a little girl and had just come home from a friend's house where my playmate's grandmother had baked us chocolate chip cookies, I asked Mom why I didn't have a grandmother too. At first, she ignored my questions, but when I kept on badgering her, she finally told me that all of our relatives in Hungary had been killed by bombs during the war. Then a faraway look came into her eyes and she seemed to forget that I was there, standing right in front of her. When she broke down and began to sob, I became frightened. I had never seen my mother cry before. I tried to comfort her by patting her face and hands, but she wouldn't stop weeping. In the end, she'd had to lie down in a darkened room with one of her headaches. Even as a six-year-old, I knew better than to disturb her when she was having a migraine. That night, Dad had come into my room, put me on his knee, and told me not to ask any more questions about the past.

"Don't bother your little head with things that happened such a long time ago, Alexandra. They're not important," he'd said. "Focus on the present, on what's happening to you right now and on what you'll be doing in the future. We're very lucky to be living in a place where everything is possible."

Dad was always more demanding of me than Mom. He pushed me hard to do well in everything, especially school. If I got 85 percent instead of 90 on a science test or a B instead of an A on an English essay, he'd insist I study harder the next time. "Remember, Alexandra," he always told me, "knowledge is the only thing they can't take away from you."

As I got older, I realized that in his own way, Dad was as secretive as Mom, and I soon learned that any questions about their lives in the old country would get me one of his speeches and one of her headaches. So I just left closed the book that contained the story of my parents' lives in that small country on the other side of the ocean. After a while, I began to believe that that story had nothing to do with me. I even forgot to be curious about it. Every now and again, however, their surprising reactions to unremarkable events reminded me of the censored chapter in their lives. This was definitely one of those times. But it didn't take a genius to figure out from Mom's firm expression that she was not about to explain why my Girl Guide uniform had startled her.

"Hurry up!" she said, cutting me off before I could even start to ask her any questions. "Molly and her father will be here any minute. You must have something to eat before you go."

I bolted down most of the food on my plate but didn't touch the dark rye toast, so different from the white Wonder Bread my friends had for breakfast. I could hear honking outside.

"They're here. I'd better go."

"Take your toast with you," Mom said.

"I don't want it. I'm too fat."

"Nonsense! You're the right weight, just what you should be. Finish it in the car."

The honking outside intensified. I grabbed for the toast and knocked it to the kitchen floor. Mom bent down, picked it up, and kissed it before putting it back on the table. As long as I could remember, she'd done this whenever a piece of bread fell to the ground. She said she was showing her gratitude that we had enough to eat.

Honking outside again.

"I've got to run!" I blew her a kiss.

"Call me as soon as you get there."

"Mom, please. Nobody calls her parents!"

I kissed her goodbye properly and rushed through the door to the humongous brand-new 1960 Plymouth humming by the curb.

It took only a few minutes for us to arrive at the River Heights Community Center on tree-lined Corydon Road. After saying a quick goodbye to Molly's father, we joined the groups of girls descending the stone steps to the meeting room in the basement of the building. The large hall was buzzing with the chatter of at least fifty girls of different shapes, sizes, and ages, all dressed in their Girl Guide uniforms. A large banner decorated the back wall of the room. "Welcome to Girl Guide Company No. 2!" it announced in bold black letters.

"Come on!" Molly said, tugging on my arm. "I want to introduce you to our captain and our patrol leader." She led me to a smiling middle-aged woman with salt-and-pepper hair. The woman was dressed in a dark blue uniform, just like us. Beside her stood a pretty girl with a long ponytail. Her name, I knew, was Christie Sutherland, and she was the most popular girl in our school. She usually ignored me, but today she gave a frosty little smile.

"Mrs. Cowan, Christie, I'd like you to meet Alexandra Gal. She wants to join our company," Molly said. "Alex wants to be in the Canaries with us, Christie."

"Welcome aboard!" Mrs. Cowan said.

"Why didn't you join us when your friends did?" was Christie's greeting.

"Alex had piano lessons on Saturday mornings," Molly said, answering before I got the chance. "It took her this long to talk her mother into letting her quit them."

A shiver of guilt ran down my spine when I thought of all the nagging I'd had to do before Mom gave in. She played the piano beautifully, and my musical education was important to her. Only when both Dad and my teacher had convinced her that I'd never become a concert pianist did she agree to my giving up music. I found it hard to believe, but I was finally free of the piano I hated.

"I'm sure that Molly will be happy to show you around, my dear. I'll catch up with you later," Mrs. Cowan said before turning to another girl who had just come into the meeting room.

Molly led me to a kitchen in the corner of the hall. Christie followed us. A large white refrigerator, a stove, and a small countertop were lined up along the wall, with painted white cabinets directly above. The two other members of the Canary patrol were sitting cross-legged on the linoleum floor. The three of us sat down beside them.

"Look who I've brought with me," Molly said to them.

One of the girls was Jean McCormick, my other best friend. She let out a whoop of delight. "You didn't tell me that you were joining Guides!" she shrieked.

"I wanted to surprise you."

"I guess you know everybody here," Molly said.

"She doesn't know me," said a tiny girl with a halo of red hair and a friendly smile. "My name's Isabel."

"I'm Alex Gal. Nice to meet you." I noticed she held a pad of paper and a pencil in her hand. "What are you doing?"

"The Canaries will be hosting the annual tea this year, as part of our work for our hostess badges," she said. "That means that we're responsible for organizing the tea. Our mothers and all of the girls in our company will be invited to it. We'll be baking cookies and cakes and making punch. The younger girls in our troop can also do some baking if they want to, but we're in charge. Our mothers are allowed to advise us, of course, but we have to do everything ourselves. We already began planning the party at our last meeting," she added.

"We'll even be drawing our own party invitations," Jean said. "And –"

The tinkling of a bell and the clapping of hands cut her off mid-sentence. The gaggle of Guides fell silent.

"Attention, girls!" Mrs. Cowan cried. For such a small lady, she had a mighty voice. "Line up, please."

With practiced ease, even the youngest members formed themselves into a straight line and marched into an open horseshoe formation. I tagged along behind Molly, trying not to stumble over my own feet.

"Color party, fall out!" called Mrs. Cowan.

Two girls stepped forward – Christie Sutherland, our patrol leader, was on the left and Jean, her second, was on the right. Mrs. Cowan took the red-and-blue Union Jack out of a stand and handed it to Christie. She and Jean then turned smartly and marched to one end of the horseshoe, where they turned again and faced the rest of the company. Next, we all recited the Girl Guide motto. I was lost after the phrase "A guide is always pre-pared" but promised myself to memorize the rest as soon as possible. Then we sat down on the carpet and took attendance. A piggy bank was passed around and each girl dropped a dime into it with a hard ping.

"I'd like to welcome a new member to our company – Alexandra Gal," Mrs. Cowan announced. "She has joined the Canary patrol. Let's give Alexandra a proper Girl Guide welcome!"

All of the girls clapped enthusiastically, and the ones nearest me patted me on the back.

"I have some more wonderful news to share with you," added Mrs. Cowan in a pleased tone. "As you already know, I announced last week that we'd be holding our annual tea on Saturday, November 21. The Canaries will be in charge, and they are already hard at work planning the menu," she said, smiling at us. "In the past, our annual teas have taken place in this hall." She waved her hands in all directions. "But this year, I decided to investigate the possibility of using a more glamorous location."

All our eyes were fixed on her. She took a deep breath and announced dramatically: "I spoke to the catering manager of the Sports Club, and he has agreed to allow us to hold our tea in the banquet hall, free of charge, if we provide our own refreshments."

A ripple of excitement passed through the room.

"Dad plays tennis there every week," I whispered to Molly, "but I've never been. He doesn't take Mom or me with him."

"The club is a very elegant facility," Mrs. Cowan continued. "Very elegant indeed! I think you'll all agree that we're lucky to have the opportunity to use the hall. So all those in favor of having our tea at the Sports Club, put your hands up."

Arms shot up into the air. An excited mumur filled the room.

"Excellent. I'll call the manager first thing Monday morning and firm up the date. Now, I'm sure you all want to get back to work on your badges," she said, "especially the Canaries. So . . . color party, fall out!"

A few minutes later, all the Canaries, including the two flag-bearers, were once again huddled in the corner of the room, by the kitchen.

"We're lucky," Jean said. "We'll be the hostesses for the most elegant tea our company has ever had. If we run into any problems, Mrs. Cowan will help us. She's really nice."

"Let's explain our plans to Alex," Christie said. "Each of us is expected to bake a cake or something. Then we all have other jobs on top of that. I'm responsible for the invitations."

"Isabel and I will be making party sandwiches," Jean offered, nodding in her friend's direction.

"I'm in charge of decorations," Molly said. "Do you want to help me?"

"I'd love to. I have two rolls of crepe-paper streamers left over from our last birthday party," I said, looking at Jean. We were both born at the end of November and always celebrated our birthdays with a joint party. "I can bring the decorations with me to next week's meeting," I offered.

"For sure! Most of the work is done the day before the tea, but we have to organize our supplies," Molly said. "You should also decide what you want to bake."

"I'll talk to my mother. She has a lot of good recipes."

Just then, Christie glanced at her watch and jumped up. "It's almost noon," she said. She walked to the center of the hall and called out, "Campfire time!"

With the familiarity of custom, the entire company gathered in a circle and launched into "God Save the Queen." Then we sat on the floor and linked hands. In the center of the circle, joined to a plug in the wall by a long cord, was a single lightbulb encircled by orange crepe-paper flames. Piles of twigs surrounded it on all four sides, making a splendid indoor campfire. My mind was full of silvery lakes, canoes, and sizzling marshmallows toasted over real campfires, but I came back to earth when the rest of the company started singing the closing song:

Day is done, gone the sun,
From the lake, from the hills, from the sky,
All is well, safely rest,
God is nigh.

A sense of warmth and fellowship and peace entered my heart. The feeling dissipated only when Mrs. Cowan had dismissed the company and we'd all spilled out into the bright afternoon sunshine.

"It's so mild that I can't believe school will be starting in a couple of days," Christie said, groaning.

"I could use another month of holidays," Jean said.

"You mean *two* months!" Molly cried.

We all laughed, breaking into smaller groups to head for home.

"I'm glad you finally joined Guides, Alex," said Molly as we waved goodbye to Christie and Jean. "I hope you'll come to camp at Caddy Lake with us next summer. It's so much fun!"

"If Mom and Dad will let me." Though I didn't say so, I thought that was unlikely. I wasn't even allowed to sleep over at friends'.

We soon reached my house, and I was already on the flagstone walk leading to the front door when Molly called after me: "We'll pick you up for Sunday school at the usual time."

Like me, she attended Sunday school and Mass at St. Stephen's Roman Catholic Church. Religion wasn't a big deal in our family, so I usually went to church with Molly and her parents, instead of my own.

As I opened the front door and entered the foyer, I came face to face with my father and his friend Dr. Wolfe.

They were leaving for their weekly tennis game at the Sports Club.

On his way out, Dad paused and gave me a hug.

"How was your meeting, Alexandra?"

"A lot of fun, Dad."

"Better than piano lessons?" he asked, winking at me.

"Much better!" I winked back.

"You'll have to tell me all about it tonight. Mom's in the kitchen making lunch for you."

"Hurry up," Dr. Wolfe said to Dad. "The sooner we get there, the sooner I can beat you."

Dad laughed, slapping his tennis racket against his thigh. "In your dreams, old buddy," he said, following his friend out of our house. "In your dreams."

Chapter 3

On the first day of school, I was almost late for my social studies class. I slipped into the room just before the bell rang and saw Molly waving to me from the back of the class.

"I saved you a seat," she said as I plopped down beside her.

Jean was in the row in front of us. She turned around and, in a sarcastic voice, asked, "Aren't you happy to be back at school?"

I stuck out my tongue.

"We're going to be so busy with homework and planning our tea for Girl Guides," Molly said, a little glumly.

Jean smiled. "I'm so glad you joined, Alex. You're going to love it. All the girls are really nice – except Christie, of course. She's such a snob."

"Did she invite you to her birthday party?" Molly asked me.

"She'd never invite me!" The ever-popular Christie barely acknowledged my existence when we passed each other in the hall. "She doesn't even know I'm alive."

"Me neither," Molly said.

"Or me," Jean said. "Well, never mind. Fall is here, so we can start planning our own birthday party soon."

"It's still too early – almost three months away. I don't think . . ." My voice trailed off as the classroom door opened and a blond boy sauntered into the room. My heart began tap dancing in my chest when he sat down in an empty seat at the end of our row.

Molly nudged me with her elbow. "The boy from the beach!"

Jean turned around again. "His name's Jacob Pearlman. I heard Miss Wilton telling Mr. Jackson that he just moved here from Toronto."

"You were right, Alex," said Molly. "He is *seriously* cute!"

"Wait! I just realized something," Jean whispered. "If he's the same boy who went back to Jew beach, he mu –"

"Quiet!" Mr. Bradford said, pointing his ruler at us. "Pay attention, girls. Class is about to begin." He softened his words with a smile, and I smiled back. He was my favorite teacher, the only one who never yelled at us, strapped us, or sent us to the office.

Looking around the room, he said, "Welcome back, everybody. It's nice to see so many familiar faces – and some new ones too." This last remark was directed at Jacob. "I know you're all eager to hit the books, so let's not waste any time. We're going to start the year by examining our country's role in the Second World War. Who can tell me the dates of the war?"

Total silence reigned in the classroom. All of us were careful not to make eye contact with him.

He laughed. "Come on! Surely one of you must know the answer. It wasn't all *that* long ago."

A couple of kids snickered in the back of the room, but no one else budged. I was on the verge of raising my arm when Jacob put up his hand.

"The Second World War started in 1939 and ended in '45," he said. "Fifteen years ago."

"Quite right, Jacob. If your classmates had cracked their textbooks at all over the summer, they too would have been able to answer my question."

Jacob gulped. Being singled out for praise by a teacher

did not enhance a person's popularity, especially in a new school.

"Who, besides Jacob, can name our allies and our foes during the war?" Mr. Bradford asked.

I put up my hand. "Germany was our enemy, and Britain, the United States, and the USSR were our allies." Jacob wasn't the only one who read the social studies text.

"As usual, Alexandra has the correct answer," Mr. Bradford said, beaming at me.

I sank down in my seat, wanting to die. Mr. Bradford had a certain enthusiastic "teachery" expression on his face that always appeared when a class discussion was going well.

"Can anyone tell me the name of the leader of Germany during the war?" he asked, pacing up and down at the front of the classroom with excitement.

"Adolf Hitler," Molly said. Like me, she always made the honor roll. "Hitler was a wicked man. He picked on the Jewish people."

Jacob's arm shot up. "Picked on them?" he cried out, even before the teacher gave him permission to speak. "Hitler did much more than pick on the Jews. He put them into concentration camps, then gassed millions and millions of them. Everybody knows what Hitler did, but nobody wants to talk about it."

Molly caught her breath like someone who'd just been slapped in the face. The rest of the class fell silent. Jacob had to be mistaken. Nobody could be that evil.

"You must be wrong," I said. "Our textbook says that Hitler didn't like Jews, but no mention is made of killing people. Nobody would do something so horrible."

Jacob turned toward me. I could see recognition dawn in his eyes. "I'm telling you the complete truth," he said. "I know our textbook isn't saying what really happened because I've done a lot of reading on this subject on my own. Hitler even murdered members of my own family who lived in Europe during the war."

Some of the kids shifted uneasily in their seats. But nobody, not even Mr. Bradford, uttered a sound. We all just stared at Jacob. The war was no longer a bunch of statistics or a few dry paragraphs in our textbook. I thought of bombs and fires and dead people, even kids my own age. Kids who were like me, who once had spent their days going to school and hanging around with their friends.

Finally, Mr. Bradford cleared his throat. "Unfortunately, class, what Jacob says is true. I have seen newsreels of the terrible atrocities committed in the camps against the Jewish people, just as Jacob describes. These events were so awful that most people are reluctant to discuss them, I'm afraid, and our textbook doesn't mention at all the suffering of the Jewish people during the war." He sighed sadly. "Perhaps we should just leave this discussion there for now. We'll continue on with it next class. For now, let's all take out our textbooks and read quietly until the bell rings."

A chorus of deep groans greeted his words, but everyone did as he asked. In what seemed like no time, the bell was ringing and the class was over. Students started collecting their books and leaving the room as quickly as possible.

Jacob, like everyone else, was gathering up his books. When I waved and called out, he walked over to my desk. I noticed that he towered over me, even though I was one of the tallest girls in our class.

"Hi," he said shyly. "Do you remember me from the beach?"

"I sure do! I didn't know you'd be in my school, though."

"Neither did I. My name's Jacob. Jacob Pearlman."

"I'm Alexandra, but my friends call me Alex," I said, favoring him with my best smile. "And these are my friends Molly and Jean."

He grinned back. "Hi," he said. He really did have the cutest dimples I had ever seen. "I hope I didn't embarrass you in class, but the war is personal to me." He was talking to Molly and Jean too, but he looked only at me.

"I wish I knew more about it," I said quietly. "My parents were also in Europe during the war, but they never talk about their experiences."

"You should ask them," Jacob said.

"I have, many times, but they won't tell me anything."

"Well, keep on asking until they *will* tell you."

"Ahem," Molly said, interrupting us with a smirk on her face. "I've got math next period, so I have to hurry." She gestured to Jean, who trailed after her in silence.

As Jacob and I turned to follow them to the door, Mr. Bradford motioned us over to his desk.

"Interesting discussion, you two. I can see that you'll be a valuable addition to our class, Jacob," he said, nodding his head. "I'm glad you spoke up. Our textbook is inadequate in many ways," he added as he waved us out of the room.

When we got into the hallway, we stood awkwardly for a moment, Jacob polishing the gray linoleum floor with the toe of his shoe.

"Well, I'm off to math class too," I said with more confidence than I felt. "Where are you going?"

"I've got French next," Jacob said, his eyes fixed on the floor.

"I'd offer to show you the way, but the French room is just around the corner. And anyway, Madame Appelle

doesn't let you speak a word of English once you get anywhere near her classroom."

Jacob laughed. "Then she won't get much sense out of
me. French is my worst subject." He continued to stare
at the floor. "It's too bad you're not in my class."

"I have French in the afternoon." The bell rang again.
"Oops," I said, "I'd better get going or I'll be late."

He called after me when I was already halfway down
the hall. "Alex!" he said. "Do you live nearby? I can walk
you home after school."

"Sure." I felt too shy to look at him.

"I'll wait for you in front of the gym. See you later!"

I floated the rest of the way to the math room, certain
that my feet didn't even touch the ground.

Chapter 4

❋❋❋❋❋❋❋❋❋❋❋❋❋❋❋❋❋❋❋❋❋❋❋❋❋❋❋❋❋❋

Jacob walked me home every day during the first week of school. He even asked me to go for a walk with him on Saturday afternoon. I didn't tell Mom about his invitation because I was worried that she would say I was too young to meet a boy. It wasn't really lying, I told myself, but just keeping a secret.

As I was getting ready to meet Jacob, I stared at myself in the mirror in my room. I knew I was looking my best. My blonde curly hair was pulled back into a ponytail, and my pink blouse with the sweetheart collar was pretty. A swingy black skirt with a wide, black patent belt completed my outfit.

When I went downstairs to tell my parents that I was

going out, I found Mom in an easy chair, reading the paper. Dad was sprawled out on the couch, taking a nap. Mom put her finger to her lips, nodding her head in Dad's direction.

"I'll be home in a couple of hours," I whispered. "I'm going for a walk with a friend."

"Take a sweater. It cools down quickly," Mom said before returning to her paper.

Instead of arguing, I grabbed a sweater and made my escape as quickly as possible. I just wanted to get out of the house before she could ask which friend I was meeting.

As I came down the front steps, I could see Jacob waiting for me at the end of the street. He had taken off his jacket, and I knew right away that my sweater would be too warm, even if I left it open. I didn't care, though. I was just happy to be spending the afternoon with him.

"This neighborhood reminds me of our street in Toronto," Jacob said as I approached. He was looking around at the old homes on both sides of the street.

"It must have been rough leaving your friends."

"I was upset when Dad announced that we'd be moving," he admitted. "But he inherited a dry-cleaner's shop from his cousin. He says it's a good opportunity for our family, one we can't afford to pass up."

"Which is your shop?"

"It's called Freddy's Dry-Cleaning Emporium."

"You're kidding! We get all of our dry-cleaning done there."

"I thought you might, since we're almost neighbors," Jacob said. "Our apartment is above the shop." He sighed. "I miss my friends back home, though. We've been together since kindergarten." He shifted his jacket to his other arm, and the dimple by his mouth deepened as he looked at me. "However, I can see that moving has certain advantages."

I searched my mind wildly for a clever reply but could think of nothing to say. I was relieved when I saw a yard sale sign in front of a large white house across the street from us. "Let's see what they're selling!" I cried.

The entire front lawn was littered with large boxes, the type used in stores to pack groceries. One was full of boots and shoes of every color and style. Another was loaded with electric tools, while a third one held pots and pans. A kitchen table had been set up right in front of the house. A middle-aged woman with crimped gray hair was sitting on a chair behind the table. Despite the mild weather, she wore a trench coat buttoned high up her neck. We were her only customers. It took me a minute to recognize her out of uniform, but then I saw that it was Mrs. Cowan, my Girl Guide leader.

"You'll find lots of bargains here," she said in greeting.

Then she peered at me intently. "Don't I know you? You look familiar."

"I'm Alexandra Gal. I joined your Guide troop last week – the Canary patrol."

"Yes, of course. Did you enjoy yourself, dear?" she asked.

"I had a good time. Thanks," I said, nodding. "Is it okay if we look around?"

"That's why I'm here," she said. "Take your time. I have lots of nice things for sale."

Several shoeboxes full of different objects were lined up on the table in front of her. One contained buttons of various shapes and sizes. Another held a pile of costume jewelry. I picked up a pretty bracelet made of brightly colored beads.

"Can I try it on?" I asked Mrs. Cowan.

"Go ahead," she said. Turning to Jacob, she added, "It would make a nice gift for your girlfriend."

"He's not –"

Jacob rolled his eyes and motioned for me to keep quiet. "You never know what'll happen," he whispered. "You might be my girlfriend someday." His ears had turned bright red.

The bracelet was pretty on my wrist. I held up my arm for Jacob to see.

"It's nice," he said. "I'll buy it for you."

"Oh no! I don't think —"

"I really want to," he said, interrupting me. "A getting-to-know-you present. How much is the bracelet?" he asked Mrs. Cowan.

"You can have it for fifty cents."

"It's too much," I whispered to him. "It's not worth more than a quarter."

"Are you sure?"

"I can buy one brand new at Eaton's for the same price." I pulled it off my wrist and gave it back to him.

"Still, it's very pretty," he said. He twirled it around in his hand before turning back to Mrs. Cowan. "We like your bracelet, but the price is too high. Can you sell it to me for a quarter?"

"Come on, young man," she said with a smile. "My prices are fair. Why are you trying to jew me down?"

The bracelet fell out of Jacob's hand and onto the tabletop with a loud thunk. The color ran out of his face, and his mouth opened and closed convulsively several times, though no sound came out.

"How dare you talk to me like that," he finally said in a quiet voice.

"What do you mean?" Mrs. Cowan asked. She seemed genuinely puzzled. "What did I say?"

Like her, I couldn't understand why he was so upset. "What's wrong, Jacob?" I asked.

He didn't answer me. He just stared at Mrs. Cowan for a long moment, then he waved his hand in frustration. "You're an ignorant person!" he spat. "And you should watch what you say." He turned and headed toward the street. "Come on, Alex. Let's go!"

I looked at Mrs. Cowan and threw up my hands in confusion. I could see by her expression that she shared my bewilderment. As I trailed after Jacob, her voice rang in my ears. "Come back!" she cried. "What's the matter with you? Why are you so angry?"

I stole a look at Jacob's stricken face. "I don't understand why you're so mad either," I said. "She didn't say anything so terrible."

"How can you say that, Alex? Don't you understand what the phrase 'jew me down' means?"

I shrugged. "It's just an expression. Everybody uses it when they don't want you to haggle." I didn't dare tell him that my friends and I said it all the time.

"It's an insult," Jacob said. He was shaking with fury. "Don't you realize that it demeans Jewish people? That it implies that we're cheap?"

I stopped dead in my tracks. "Jacob, I'm *so* sorry! I never thought about what the term meant."

"Nobody does. The world is full of stupid people."

I touched his arm to comfort him, but he would not be consoled.

"It's not fair, Alex. She didn't even realize that what she was saying was offensive. Neither did you! That's the worst of all."

"I don't know what to say, Jacob. I didn't understand. . . . I won't make the same mistake again."

He sighed deeply, but I could feel him relaxing. We walked along in silence for a few moments, and I racked my brains for some way to make things up to him. I felt so bad that I did something I'd never had the nerve to do before. "Will you come with me to the school dance next Friday?" I asked.

His face brightened immediately. "I'd love to. When should I pick you up?"

"It's at seven, but nobody gets there till after eight."

He grabbed my hand, and a million butterflies began to dance in my stomach. "Come to my house for Shabbos dinner," he said. "Afterward, my father will drive us to the dance."

"Shabbos dinner?"

He laughed. "I forgot that you wouldn't know what I'm talking about. I meant Friday night dinner. Come, you'll like it."

"I'll have to check with Mom and Dad, but I'm sure it'll be okay with them."

I'll make sure it's all right, I said to myself. It was time Mom and Dad realized that I was no longer a baby.

Chapter 5

❊❊❊❊❊❊❊❊❊❊❊❊❊❊❊❊❊❊❊❊❊❊❊❊❊

Jean and Molly came over to my house after dinner on Saturday night, as usual, so we could do our homework together. We always met at my house on weekends because my parents went to the movies most Saturday nights and we knew we would be alone. Dad said it did Mom good to get out of the house, since she never went anywhere by herself during the week while he was at work.

That night, the three of us were lying on the carpet in my room, trying to finish the geometry problems our math teacher, Miss Wilton, had assigned.

"Does one of you have the answer to the last question? What's an isosceles triangle?" Molly asked.

"A triangle with two equal opposite sides," Jean said.

Molly and I copied the answer into our notebooks before shutting them closed.

"Finished at last!" Molly said, stretching her arms wide. "Now we can talk. So tell us, Alex, what are you wearing to the dance?"

"My new dress." I opened the closet and pulled the dress off a hanger. My fingers caressed the soft material, a deep green that made my skin look whiter and my hair blonder. "I've only worn it once before, for my parents' anniversary."

"Try it on for us," Jean said.

I pulled off the blouse and skirt I was wearing and slipped on the dress. Molly zipped me up, and I peered into my dresser mirror. The tight bodice and long cuffed sleeves were very fashionable. The wide skirt fanned out in a satisfying manner as I twirled around, my bouncing ponytail keeping rhythm.

"What's that on your cuff?" Molly asked.

I lifted my arm to look at the brownish stain she was pointing to.

"Oh no! It must be a grease stain. I'll ask Mom to take the dress to the dry-cleaners. It'll give her a chance to meet Jacob's parents." I twirled around again. "It's a pretty dress, isn't it?"

"It's beautiful," Jean said. "You look so nice."

"You do," Molly agreed. "But you could use a scarf around the neckline – something green."

I examined my reflection carefully. Molly was right. The round neckline was very plain. "A scarf *would* look good. I know exactly the one I want, too. Dad gave Mom a beautiful green silk scarf for their anniversary. It'll go perfectly with my dress. She keeps it in her dresser in their bedroom. Let's go get it!"

"Won't your mother be mad if you take her scarf?" Jean asked.

"Not if she doesn't find out," I told her. "I'll put it on at Jacob's house."

Jean shook her head but followed Molly and me into my parents' bedroom. Before tackling Mom's dresser, we examined the bottles of potions and tubes of lipstick arranged in neat rows on top of her dressing table. I chose a tube in a Moonlight Pink shade and started applying it. Molly put on Passionate Red, while Jean's lips were Slightly Burgundy. Each one of us also sprayed Chanel No. 5 cologne on the inside of our wrists.

Finally, I pulled out the bottom drawer of the dresser. There it was – Mom's new scarf. As I picked it up, I saw that a flat package wrapped in tissue paper was hidden below it. Although the paper was creased, as if it had been unwrapped and rewrapped many times, I was very careful while opening it. Inside was a slim, rectangular book. It had a stained cover with a picture of two Mounties on horseback. It was obvious that the crimson uniforms and wide-brimmed hats of the Mounties and the shiny black coats of their horses had been hand-colored. Above the picture was the title in bold, dark letters. *Canada*, it said.

I opened the book and leafed through it. At a quick glance, it seemed to be a history of the country. It was filled with black-and-white photographs and drawings. I recognized the Rocky Mountains and the Parliament Buildings in Ottawa. I saw a drawing of the Selkirk settlers in their covered wagons and one of British soldiers fighting a band of fierce Natives.

"What have you got there?" Molly asked, reaching for the book.

As I handed it to her, two black-and-white photographs with wavy edges fell from among its pages and fluttered to the floor. I stooped down and carefully picked them up. The pictures were so faded that it was hard to see the faces of the people in them.

One of the photos showed a young woman in a short-sleeved print dress with long, light-colored hair flowing over her shoulders and a large sausage curl at her forehead. She was standing in front of a brick house with tall iron gates. She must have been around seventeen or eighteen years old. She was laughing into the camera and shading her eyes from the sun. The second photo was more formal. In it, the same girl was sitting on a bench in a garden full of large trees and bushes. The full skirt of her old-fashioned dress fanned prettily around her legs. There were three other people also in the picture. Sitting on the bench to the girl's right was a middle-aged, dark-haired woman in a long-skirted suit. On the girl's other side was a very old lady with snowy hair who was resting her feet on a small stool. Behind them all stood a younger girl with shorter dark hair. She was resting her hands on the old lady's shoulders and smiling. All of the figures in both photographs had large six-pointed stars on their clothing, right over their hearts.

"Whose pictures are these?" Jean asked.

"I don't know. I've never seen them before."

I passed the photo of the four women to Jean and the one of the girl to Molly.

"She's pretty," Molly said. "She also looks familiar." She frowned. "I wish the picture was clearer. But I'm pretty sure I've seen her somewhere before."

"Let me have another look," I said. I took the pictures out of their hands and looked at them more closely. I knew I'd never laid eyes on the two older women or the girl with the dark hair, but Molly was right about the girl with the curl over her forehead. She *was* familiar. I racked my brains but couldn't remember where I'd seen her.

Just then, the doorbell rang. We peeked out of the window.

"It's my dad!" Molly said. "He's early. We have to go." She and Jean quickly wiped the lipstick off their mouths.

When the bell pealed again, we hurried downstairs and I went to open the door.

"Don't tell anybody about the pictures," I whispered as they left. "Mom will kill me if she finds out I was snooping in her dresser."

After I'd locked the door behind them, I went back to my parents' room, sank down on their bed, and leafed through the book again. It was definitely a history of Canada. But the photographs aroused my curiosity much more. I picked them up again, wishing they weren't so faded. The women in them smiled back at me as before. When I turned the pictures over, I saw that their backs, like their fronts, were yellowed and stained. Someone had written a few words on each one in faded but still legible handwriting. "Agi, June 1944" was on the back of the picture of the young girl. What a strange coincidence! Mom's name was Agi too. Well, her name was Agnes, but Dad always called her Agi. She was the only Agi I'd ever heard of.

I looked at the other photo. The same hand had written, "Agi, Mama Lotti, Jutka, and me, June 1944." Once again, only the name Agi was familiar. Who was the Agi in the picture? Who were the women she was sitting with? Why did all of them have stars on their dresses? And most important, why had Mom hidden these photographs away among her clothes?

I had a lot of questions to ask her, but I knew she'd be furious if she found out that I'd been going through her drawers. I slipped the photos back among the pages of the book and carefully rewrapped it. Then I put the package into the drawer where I had found it and covered it with her scarf, the same as before.

I looked around the room. Nothing was out of place, so I went down to the living room and watched a little TV until I began to feel tired and decided to go to bed. I must have fallen asleep right away, for I didn't even hear Mom and Dad come home.

I woke up early Sunday morning with the sun sneaking into my room through the folds of the curtains. It was so quiet that I could hear the ticking of the grandfather clock outside my bedroom and the swishing of its pendulum. Mom and Dad must have gone for their regular morning walk. Mom's bad leg stiffened up if she didn't exercise regularly, and Dad always went with her, since she never went anywhere by herself. I was drifting off to sleep once again when the chiming of the clock jolted me back awake.

I counted nine chimes. Molly would be picking me up for church in half an hour, and I wasn't even dressed! I tore off the plaid pajamas I was wearing and shrugged into a pink mohair sweater and a brown poodle skirt with a belt that cinched my waist and made it nice and small. While I was dragging a brush through my hair in a futile attempt to tame my curls, I remembered the message that Father Mike had sent to Mom last Sunday. He'd wanted her to call him about setting a date for my confirmation, and I knew he'd be unhappy when I told him Mom's response.

To make things worse, I forgot where I had put my rosary after Mass last week. I knew that Father Mike would be upset if I showed up at church without it. I looked for it first in the white leatherette jewelry box on top of my dresser. The little pink ballerina inside the lid twirled around gaily, but I couldn't see the rosary beads tangled up with my necklaces. Nor had I tossed it down on my desk or my dresser. I would have to borrow Mom's rosary. I knew she kept it in the top drawer of her dresser because I'd seen her put it there after Mass on Easter Sunday, the last time she had come to church with me.

A dark wooden bureau and a heavy dresser stood guard over my parents' bed. I had a sudden urge to turn around and march right out of their bedroom, but the thought of Father Mike's disapproval hardened my resolve. At least I wouldn't have to look for long, I thought. I walked up to the dresser and grasped the drawer handle, but then I let it go. Mom would be beside herself if she found out that I'd gone through her belongings without her permission not once but twice. She would say it was an invasion of her privacy. But there was no other way. If I wanted to find her rosary, I would have to risk her annoyance by searching through her things.

A quick spray of Chanel No. 5 lifted my spirits, then I shifted my attention to the drawers in her dresser. The top one held the lace mantilla Mom had worn to church, but there was no sign of her rosary. I pushed her monogrammed handkerchiefs aside but found nothing. Could she have put it into the second drawer? She was such a neat freak that I knew better than to be messy. I moved around her folded underwear and nylon stockings with care but still couldn't find it.

In a few brief minutes, I'd been through all the drawers except the one that held her scarf. Although I didn't remember seeing the rosary in it the day before, I thought I'd better check again, so I pulled out the drawer and rifled through its contents. There was no rosary, but

I came upon the old photographs once more and decided to have another quick look at them. I picked up the picture of the girl first. The photo was so blurred that it was hard to make out her features, but she definitely looked familiar. I stared at her face for a long moment and then it hit me. I marched over to the mirror and held the photo next to my face. My breath caught in my throat and my hands began to tremble as I realized that if I disregarded the old-fashioned clothes and the sausage curl, the girl in the picture looked exactly like the girl staring back at me in the mirror. I couldn't believe my eyes. I just stood there, frozen, staring at the photo. Then I remembered that Dad kept a magnifying glass on his desk in the den. I rushed downstairs to get it. As I peered through it, the features of the girl came into focus. There was no doubt – the face staring back at me was a slightly older carbon copy of mine.

Could the girl in the picture be my mother when she was just a little older than me? I wondered. Everybody said I looked just like her. The longer I examined the pictures, the more convinced I became that I was looking at a younger version of a Mom I had never seen before – a Mom who looked happy. I decided to ask her about the photos when I got home. I was too curious to worry about the trouble I would get into when she found out that I'd been searching in her drawers. I had to have some answers.

When the doorbell rang, I hastily shoved the photographs back where I had found them and rushed to open the door for my friend.

"We're late," Molly said as we climbed into the back seat of her parents' car.

"I couldn't find my rosary."

"We've lots of time," Mrs. Windsor said, turning around in her seat to greet me. "But we might as well get going."

She revved up the car and turned on the radio.

"I keep thinking about those photographs we found yesterday," Molly whispered behind a cupped palm. "I can't get that girl out of my mind. I have the feeling I've seen her somewhere before."

I opened my mouth to tell her about my discovery, but then I stopped myself from speaking. I'd better talk to Mom first, I thought.

"She did look familiar," I mumbled instead.

I let out a sigh of relief when Mrs. Windsor pulled up to the curb in front of the church.

"Thanks for the ride, Mrs. Windsor. My parents will take us home," I said as I climbed out of the car. "Come on, Molly. Sister Ursula will kill us if we're late."

Chapter 6

✲✲✲✲✲✲✲✲✲✲✲✲✲✲✲✲✲✲✲✲✲✲✲✲✲✲✲

The room was half full of kids by the time Molly and I slipped into our seats in the back row. Our Sunday school class was in the Catholic day school attached to our church. The large classroom, with its faded gray walls, scarred brown student desks, and battered teacher's table in front of the blackboard, reminded me of my homeroom at Lord Selkirk High. The large crucifix hanging on the wall was comfortingly familiar.

The class was filling up. It was nice to see friends we didn't see during the week.

"I didn't memorize the questions and answers for Lesson 16, did you?" Molly whispered to me just as Father Mike strode into the room. He was followed closely by Sister Ursula, famous for her pinched features, prickly chin, and wicked temper. A kind-faced older man, Father Mike was smiling in his usual benign manner, while Sister Ursula greeted us with her perpetual frown of disapproval.

"Good morning, boys and girls," Father Mike boomed in a good-natured voice. He always treated us as if we were still little kids, but we liked him so much that we didn't mind. Sister was silent, her sallow face framed by a white wimple and her bulging eyes scanning the room for possible wrongdoing. I gulped down the gum I was chewing before she noticed my transgression.

"I dropped by before Mass to make sure that all of you understood last Sunday's sermon," the priest said. "Any questions?"

No hands were raised.

"Excellent! Excellent!" He clapped his hands together in satisfaction. "I'll be off, then. See you at Mass." He turned to leave, then seemed to remember something. "Oh, may I speak to you for a moment, Alexandra?"

I stood up with a sigh. I was hoping that he'd forgotten about his message to Mom and Dad, but no such luck. I followed him into the hall.

"Well, my dear, did you speak to your parents like I asked you to? When do they want you to have your confirmation?"

"I talked to them, Father. My mother told me that confirmation is a North American custom that they didn't practice in their church in the old country, so it doesn't mean anything to them. They decided not to have me confirmed." I spoke as earnestly as I could. I didn't want the priest to think badly of my parents. "Don't forget, Father, they came to Canada not so very long ago."

He stared at me for a long, silent moment, then cleared his throat before speaking again. "I see," he finally said. "And what about you, Alexandra? Would you like to be confirmed into our church?"

"Sure, Father. Most of my friends had their confirmations ages ago. But I don't think my parents will change their minds."

He scratched his chin thoughtfully. "I haven't talked to your mother and father for a while. Tell them that I'll give them a call. Or perhaps I'll drop in at your house one evening this week. I'm sure we'll be able to reach some kind of compromise." He patted me on the shoulder. "You'd better return to your class before Sister gets annoyed."

I often felt that the priest was as afraid of the nun as the rest of us. I turned and was just opening the classroom door when he called after me once more.

"Alexandra, I believe I have something of yours." He reached into his pocket and pulled out my missing rosary.

"Oh, Father, thank you! Where did you find it? I turned the house upside down looking for it."

"It was on one of the pews in church last Sunday. I remembered seeing you with it and knew it must be yours." He waved goodbye as he set off in the direction of the church.

I slipped back into the classroom just as Sister Ursula was beginning to test us on our catechism questions. To make the lesson more difficult, she mixed up the questions instead of asking them in the order they appeared in our Baltimore Catechism books. Every one of us was careful to avoid making eye contact with her, but this was a useless exercise. Sister made sure that everybody got tested.

"What is the first commandment of God?" the nun asked, pointing her ever-present ruler at Molly, who was rapidly slipping down behind her desk.

"I don't know, Sister," Molly mumbled, shifting in her seat and chewing on a strand of her hair. "I had a science test to study for, so I had no time to –"

Her voice cut out when Sister Ursula's ruler slammed down on the edge of her desk, just a few inches from her fingers. She shrank even farther down in her seat, her face neon bright. I began to feel the fluttering grip of fear settling into the pit of my own stomach when the unrelenting tap of Sister Ursula's fingers made its way to the desktop next to mine.

"Who knows the answer?" she asked.

A girl at the front of the room put up her hand.

"The first commandment of God is 'I am the Lord thy God; thou shalt not have strange gods before Me,'" she repeated, parrot-like.

"Excellent!" Sister Ursula said, turning toward me. When she came a few steps closer, I could see three long white hairs quivering under her chin. The hairs hypnotized me like the headlights of a car do an errant deer. I couldn't take my eyes off them.

"How does a Catholic sin against faith?" she asked me.

My mind drew a blank. The straight memorization of the catechism questions was always difficult for me. I forced my attention away from Sister's chin.

"I said, how does a Catholic sin against faith?" she repeated, her words punctuated by a whoosh of her ruler.

My memory finally clicked in. "A Catholic sins against faith by not believing what God has revealed, and by taking part in non-Catholic worship."

"Very good. Always remember, children – outside of the church, outside of salvation," Sister Ursula declared in a firm voice.

As soon as Sunday school was over, our class went to Mass in the sanctuary. All of us paid close attention to Father Mike's sermon, for he knew which topics interested us. When the service ended, Molly went to the bathroom. By the time we were ready to leave the church, all of our friends had already gone. As we headed toward the front entrance, Mom and Dad came into the lobby.

"Hello, darlings," Mom said. "We were just coming to get you. We were afraid we'd missed you."

Before I could reply, the door leading to Father Mike's study swung open and a well-dressed middle-aged couple came out. They were about to pass us by when the man came to a sudden stop.

"Dr. and Mrs. Gal! It is you, isn't it?" He grabbed hold of Dad's hand and began to pump it. I could see by my parents' bewildered expressions that they had no idea who he was. "You're looking so prosperous that I almost didn't recognize you," the man said in a jovial tone. "You don't remember me, do you?" He patted his stomach. "There's a lot more of me than when you last saw me. At least ten years must have passed since you first came into my shop in Toronto."

"Of course!" Dad said, slapping his forehead with his palm. "Forgive me, Mr. McCallum. It was such a long time ago."

"Oh, Mr. McCallum! We'll never forget your kindness when we were new to the country," Mom said with a smile.

"No offense taken," he replied. "I hardly recognized you myself. I'm glad to see you looking so well. Let me introduce you to my wife, Mary," he added, gesturing to the woman by his side.

"I'd like you to meet my wife, Agi, Mrs. McCallum," Dad said. "This is our daughter, Alexandra. She was the baby we used to bring into your husband's store," he added as I nodded politely at the strangers. "And this is her friend Molly."

"Has the old neighborhood changed a lot, Mr. McCallum?" Mom asked.

"You wouldn't recognize it," said the man. "All of the immigrants have moved on, except Dr. Kohn. You were good friends with him, weren't you, Dr. Gal?"

"Yes, I was. But we lost touch."

"Well, the poor man is still struggling to make ends meet."

Dad and Mom exchanged swift glances.

"I'm sorry Dr. Kohn is having so much trouble," Dad said. "He's an excellent physician."

"I don't doubt that, but you know how stupid people can be," said Mr. McCallum. "They don't want to go to a doctor who's –"

Dad cut in. "So what brings you and your husband to our city, Mrs. McCallum?" he asked with what looked like a forced smile pasted on his face.

"We're motoring to Banff," the woman said, "and we stopped to deliver a message to Father Mike from a former parishioner who now attends our church."

"Tell me, Dr. Gal, what are you and your family doing here?" Mr. McCallum asked, waving his hand in the direction of the sanctuary. "This isn't exactly where I would have expected to find you."

Dad's face turned beet red and he swallowed hard. "Well, we've got to get going," he said. "It was nice to see you again, Mr. McCallum."

For a long moment, the man looked at Dad in confusion. Then he suddenly seemed to notice the cross around my neck. He stared at it so hard that he made me feel self-conscious and I covered it with my hands. He looked from me to Dad and then around at the church as if he'd just realized something. For some reason, he seemed embarrassed.

"Drive safely," Mom said. "The roads around Banff can be treacherous." I noticed that her hands were shaking. "Well, we're late, girls," she added, hustling us out of the building.

As soon as we were in the car, I asked, "Who were those people?"

"Mr. McCallum owns a small grocery store in Toronto. We used to shop there when we first arrived in Canada. You were too young to remember," Mom said.

I turned to Dad. "I didn't understand something he said. If your friend in Toronto is a good doctor, why doesn't he have enough patients?"

"It's nothing you need to concern yourself with," Dad said.

"And another thing – did you notice how he was staring at my cross?"

"Forget it," Dad said. I could tell by the firmness of his voice that it was useless to ask more questions. "Don't worry your head over things you don't understand."

Chapter 7

✾✾✾✾✾✾✾✾✾✾✾✾✾✾✾✾✾✾✾✾✾✾✾✾✾✾

"Lunch is in two minutes, Alexandra. The food is warming in the oven. We're having chicken paprikash – your favorite," Mom said.

We sat down around the dining-room table, which had been formally set with a lace tablecloth and cloth napkins. Unlike my friends' families, we always had the main meal in the middle of the day. In spite of the early hour, two candles burned in heavy silver candlesticks at the center of the table. These were the only valuables we had brought with us from Europe. Mom said they were precious to her because they'd belonged to my grandmother.

The chicken paprikash was just as I liked it – hot and spicy.

"You're the best cook in the world, Mom."

"I have excellent recipes. Good friends gave them to me," she said. "Leave room for the second course," she added as she put a bowl of cucumber salad on the table.

"Excellent meal, Agi," Dad said.

"Nice to be so appreciated." She laughed and then turned to me. "How was Sunday school, dear?"

"Boring. Sister Ursula is hard to take."

"She's a nun, Alexandra! Show some respect," she scolded.

"Learning doesn't always have to be entertaining," Dad said in a firm voice. "Sometimes we learn the most when we must try the hardest. Always remember that knowledge is the only thing –"

"They can't take away from you." I completed the much-repeated motto for him. "Talk about double standards, Dad! You don't go to church every week, and neither does Mom. I don't see why I have to. I never have time to sleep in. It's not fair!"

"Watch it, young lady! I won't be spoken to in such a manner." Dad seemed genuinely annoyed. "When you're my age, you'll do as you like. For now, you'll do as you're told. It's for your own good."

"Stop it, you two," Mom said. She knew Dad was angry, but I could see by the muscle twitching at the side of her mouth that she was fighting not to smile at our familiar argument. I loved it when her face was so full of mischief. It made her look just like a kid. Changing the subject, she turned to me and said, "I've been doing some thinking about your Girl Guide tea. Why don't you bake a cheesecake? They're easy to make and delicious."

"I have to do it by myself," I reminded her, "without any help."

"Let's bake one together first, to give you practice. Then you'll be able to do it by yourself."

"Can I invite Jean and Molly? It'll be fun baking together."

"Good idea. Let's do it next weekend."

"After you finish you homework," Dad said just as a great big sneeze escaped my lips. "Agi," he said, laughing, "the paprika in your chicken certainly clears our sinuses."

I reached into my skirt pocket for a Kleenex, and as I did the tips of my fingers touched the cold smoothness of my rosary beads. They reminded me of the photographs I'd found in Mom's drawer. She was in a good mood, so it seemed safe to ask her about them.

"I have to tell you something, Mom," I began. "Yesterday, when Jean and Molly came over, I tried on the scarf that Dad gave you for your anniversary. I didn't think you'd mind, as long as I put it back in your drawer," I added quickly.

"Really, Alexandra! You shouldn't –"

"I found some old photographs in the drawer."

She stopped mid-sentence, her fork halted halfway to her mouth. Two round red apples dotted her cheeks. She glanced at Dad, who had put his fork down and was listening to us.

"Did you look at them?" she asked.

"Of course I did! Who are those women, Mom? One of them looks just like you, except younger. Is it a picture of you when you were a girl? When were the photos taken? The people in them look so old-fashioned." The words just tumbled out of my mouth, and once the questions had started I couldn't make them stop. "Why do they have stars on their clothes?" I asked.

My mother's eyes filled with unshed tears. "Oh, Alexandra, I thought you knew better than to snoop in my dresser!"

"I wasn't trying to be nosy," I protested. "I just wanted to show Jean and Molly your scarf."

She sighed deeply but did not reply.

"Who are those women, Mom?" I repeated more insistently.

"I think the time has come to tell the child," Dad said.

Mom put her hands over her face. "Please, Jonah. Not yet. . . . Not ever!" She pushed herself heavily from the table and grasped the handle of her cane. "I feel one of my migraines coming on," she announced. "I'm going to lie down." She hobbled out of the room before I could stop her.

I turned to Dad. "What's going on? Why is Mom so upset? What is it that you should tell me? What do you know about those old pictures?"

He took a long drink of his soda water. "Your mother will tell you about them when she's ready."

"When will that be?"

"Later," he said and began to eat.

We finished the meal in silence. Suddenly, my favorite food tasted like sawdust in my mouth.

I barely saw my mother for the next few days. When I got home from school for lunch on Monday, I wasn't greeted by the usual mouth-watering smells coming from the kitchen. And Mom wasn't waiting for me either. Instead, a note propped up on the table said that she still had a migraine and was lying down. I didn't want to disturb her when she wasn't feeling well, but I knew that Dad would be home for his own lunch in a few minutes.

We had to eat something, so I took six eggs out of the refrigerator and beat them with a whisk to make an omelette, just as I had seen Mom do many times. I was buttering the rye bread I had toasted when Dad arrived. I showed him Mom's note. He read it but did not comment as he ladled food onto his plate.

"I made enough for Mom too," I said.

"I'll take it up to her when we've finished eating," he said.

At the end of the meal, he piled the remainder of the eggs and toast onto a plate and climbed the stairs to their bedroom. I could hear loud knocking on their door, but he was back downstairs a minute later, his color high, the plate of food still clutched in his hands.

"Your mother must be sleeping. The door is locked, and she didn't open it when I knocked." He scraped the contents of the plate into the garbage can.

I stared at him. Was this the father who was constantly lecturing me not to waste food?

When Mom stayed in her room that evening and all the next day, Dad and I took turns making sandwiches for each other. We ate them in silence because he still refused to answer any of my questions. "Your mother will talk to you when she is ready," he told me. After he'd eaten lunch, he hurried back to work while I returned to school.

That evening, after dinner, he read the newspaper in his favorite armchair while I did my homework at the dining-room table. Mom never came downstairs.

I had trouble falling asleep that night. I tossed and turned, replaying the events of the past two days. All kinds of thoughts filled my brain. I remembered how Mrs. Cowan had insulted Jacob. I was still embarrassed that I hadn't understood why he was so hurt. The scene around the dining-room table on Sunday also kept running through my mind like an old movie. Why had my mother become so upset when I asked her about the photographs? I wondered. The more I thought about it, the more convinced I became that the girl in the photos was her when she was younger.

All the heavy thinking was making me thirsty, so I decided to go downstairs to the kitchen for a glass of milk. I was surprised to see light streaming out from under my parents' door. The grandfather clock in the corner showed that it was twenty minutes past three. I tiptoed closer to their door, careful to avoid the floorboards that creaked. I could hear the murmur of voices, but no matter how hard I strained, I couldn't understand what they were saying. So I risked going even closer, pressing my ear against the bedroom door. I could still hear only the odd word of their conversation.

". . . must tell her," Dad was saying.

Mom was whispering and sobbing at the same time, so it was even more difficult to make out what she was saying. I heard her cry, "No. No! She . . . wasted," but the rest of her words were too muffled to understand.

"Alexandra . . . must . . ." I heard Dad mention my name.

"Wasted!" Mom said again, before beginning to speak in Hungarian.

Suddenly, I heard footsteps approaching, then Dad's voice, clear and close. I rushed back to my room on tiptoe, careful to close the door quietly behind me. I didn't dare turn on the light, but instead lay silently on top of my covers, listening to Dad's footsteps pass my door.

Lunch the next day was a lonely affair, but at least there was food warming in the oven. The sauerkraut with meatballs, Mom's specialty, was delicious, but I had to eat it by myself with a copy of *Seventeen* magazine propped up against the salt and pepper shakers for company. Dad arrived a few minutes later, kissed me hello, and without even taking a bite of food, climbed upstairs two steps at a time. I heard the bedroom door slam and muffled voices rise in anger. I hung around at the bottom of the stairs for a while, but when I couldn't muster the courage to follow my father, I went back to school.

Both Mom and Dad were waiting for me in the

living room when I arrived home in the afternoon. Although she was a little pale, Mom seemed to be in a good mood.

"My headache is better," she said. "Come, join us."

I sat down in an armchair.

"So, darling, what have you been up to?" she asked.

"Nothing much." I twisted a strand of hair around my finger. "Oh, Father Mike told me he'd be calling you soon," I said to her, remembering the conversation I'd had with the priest a few days earlier. "I didn't have a chance to tell you before."

"What does he want?"

"To set a date for my confirmation, I think. I told him you didn't want me confirmed."

She shot a quick glance at Dad. "Did you tell Father Mike why?" she asked.

"I told him exactly what you told me, Mom – that nobody gets confirmed in the old country, so you aren't used to the custom."

Dad lowered his paper. "Confirmation is out of the question," he said.

"I agree with you, Jonah. I couldn't bear it either. But I have to tell the priest something, don't I? What do you want me to say when he calls?"

"Tell him that we don't want Alexandra confirmed. Period. You don't have to give a reason."

The longer I listened, the angrier I became. They were talking about me as if I wasn't even there. "Why can't I be confirmed?" I finally asked. "All the kids at Sunday school were ages ago."

"This topic is not open for discussion," Mom said. "Your father and I know what's best for you." She sighed. "I'll call Father Mike tomorrow and explain." She forced a smile. "How was school today?"

"Okay."

"Answer your mother properly," Dad said.

"I don't want to talk about school. I want to know what's going on." I turned to my mother. "You have headaches that last for days. You won't discuss the old pictures. You're getting excited about Father Mike. What's the matter with you?"

I was sorry as soon as the words had escaped my mouth, for her eyes quickly filled with tears.

"Nothing's the matter, darling," she whispered. "It's just that . . ." Her voice trailed off.

"Stop upsetting your mother!" Dad jumped in. "She'll explain everything to you when she is ready."

We sat in silence for the next few minutes. "So, darling," Mom finally said, "what are your plans for the weekend? Isn't your school dance on Friday? Are you and Molly going together?"

"I'll drive you," Dad said.

I kept my voice casual. "That's okay. I'm going with another friend, and I've been invited for dinner before the dance."

Mom's face brightened. "Isn't that nice. Was it Jean who asked you?"

I fixed my eyes on the carpet. My cheeks felt hot, a sure sign that a major blush was about to follow. "There's a new boy in my class. His name's Jacob, and he wants me to come to his house for Friday night dinner. His father will drive us to the dance afterward."

"It's out of the question," Dad said. "You're too young."

"Dad's right, darling," Mom said. "You're only thirteen, much too young to be going out with a boy."

"It's just dinner at a friend's house." I tried to speak in a reasonable tone, though I was silently thanking my lucky stars that they didn't know about my walks with Jacob. "Please let me go! Jacob's parents are very nice," I pleaded, casting an imploring glance in Mom's direction.

"I'm sure they are." She seemed to be thinking things over. "What do you think, Jonah?"

Dad's face softened. "If you agree, Agi, I'll go along with your decision." He turned to me. "You may go to this boy's house for dinner, and to the dance afterward, but only this once."

"Oh, thank you!" I jumped up and kissed them both.

"Wear your new dress," Mom said. "It looks very pretty on you."

"There's a stain on one of the cuffs."

Mom sighed. "You should be more careful with your clothes, dear. I'll take it to Freddy's for you. I just hope the new owners are as good as poor Freddy was."

I burst out laughing. "You'll be meeting Jacob's parents, then. Freddy was Jacob's father's uncle. When he died, he left his shop to Jacob's father. That's why they moved here."

"But Freddy was Jewish," Mom said.

"So is Jacob. That's why he invited me to his house on Friday night. His family always has a special dinner on Friday."

"Shabbos dinner," Mom whispered.

"How did you know that's what Jewish people call their Friday night dinner?"

Mom bit her lip and was silent for a long moment. "You must refuse the invitation," she finally said in a hoarse voice. "You must not go."

"Agi, we already gave our permission," Dad said.

"She must not go," Mom repeated.

I jumped up from my seat. "You never want me to go anywhere!" I cried. "You don't know what it's like to have friends!"

"Sit down, please," she said. "I do know, and I also know what it feels like to have a boy ask you out for the first time." She patted my arm. "Please, dear, sit down."

I lowered myself back into my chair. "Please, Mom! Please, Dad! Let me go."

"We already told her she could go," Dad said. "Be reasonable, Agi."

"But, Jonah, it's Shabbos dinner."

"I'm sure the . . . er, what's their name, Alex?"

"Pearlman."

"I'm sure the Pearlmans are perfectly respectable people. There's nothing wrong with her going to their house."

"But Shabbos dinner!" Mom repeated.

"If you won't let her go, you must explain why," Dad said.

Mom gave a shuddering sigh. There was an almost palpable cloud of unhappiness surrounding her. "You may tell your friend, Alexandra," she finally said in a melancholy voice, "that you can have dinner with his family."

I bit my lip to keep my tears from falling. "What's going on, Mom? I've never seen you act like this. You're scaring me!"

"Agi, can't you see that it's time for Alexandra to be told the truth?" Dad asked.

"Mom, please tell me what's wrong!" I sounded desperate even to my own ears.

She squared her shoulders. "I can't, my darling. Not yet. Give me time." She got up from the sofa and hobbled over to my chair to kiss me on the forehead. "Be patient with your old mother," she said. "I have a lot of thinking to do."

Chapter 8

❋❋❋❋❋❋❋❋❋❋❋❋❋❋❋❋❋❋❋❋❋❋❋❋❋❋❋❋

Our teachers had a staff meeting on Friday afternoon, so we were let out of school early. As I hurried home, I realized that I had forgotten to give Mom the note about the early dismissal. It didn't really matter because I had my own key, and anyway she was always home.

I let myself into the house. Through the kitchen door, I could hear my mother talking to somebody in a strange language. I was fairly certain it wasn't Hungarian, which I usually recognized, but some other language I'd never heard before.

I peered around the doorframe and saw Mom standing beside the kitchen table, her hands fluttering over the bright flame of two tapers in my grandmother's candle-sticks. Her eyes were closed and her hair was covered by a scarf. At the sound of my footsteps, she spun toward me, her face white and full of surprise.

"Hi, Mom. What are you doing?"

"Nothing . . . nothing," she stammered. "I was just praying."

"But you never pray! And why is your head covered?"

She didn't meet my eyes. "Covering our heads was an old custom in my church back home."

"Well, what language were you speaking? It didn't sound like Hungarian."

"I was using an old dialect my mother taught me. I'll teach it to you when you're older." She blew out the flames and put the candlesticks into a cupboard. "Why are you so early?"

"The teachers had a meeting. I forgot to give you the note."

She sighed. "Alexandra, you must become more responsible." She looked at me and smiled. "Take your books upstairs. I'll get you something to eat in the mean-time. I baked some cookies for you today."

I ran up to my room, dropped my school bag to the floor, and went to my closet to take out the dress I was going to wear that night. Molly was coming over, and I wanted to try it on for her. But the dress wasn't in the closet. I pushed aside all of the hangers and looked more carefully. Mom always hung my dry-cleaned clothes in my closet after she picked them up from Freddy's, but the dress definitely wasn't there.

I bounded back down the stairs two at a time. She was at the kitchen table, reading and smoking. A plate of cookies and a glass of milk were waiting for me.

"Where's my new dress?" I asked. "I can't find it anywhere."

She looked up reluctantly, her index finger separating the pages of her book. "You'll have to wear something else," she said. "Your father was held up at the office, and Freddy's was closed by the time he got home."

"Why didn't you go by yourself?" I yelled. "It's so close by that you could have walked there. You know how important this is to me!"

"And you know that I never go anywhere by myself," she said in a calm voice.

"Well, you should! All of my friends' mothers do. Why can't you be like them?" I cried.

She looked at me for a long moment. "Because I am not," she said simply, before returning to her book as if I wasn't even in the room.

I stood in front of her, shaking with fury. But when I saw that she was intent on ignoring me, I turned and stormed upstairs. Once I was in my room, I sat down on the edge of my bed, taking deep breaths to calm down. Then I stood up and walked over to my closet to choose another dress to wear. I couldn't make up my mind, though, so I decided to wait for Molly and ask her opinion. Gradually, I began to feel guilty for yelling at Mom, so I went downstairs to apologize. I found her in the living room, at the piano, her fingers caressing the keys, her eyes closed, her face full of emotion. I could see that she was a million miles away.

"I'm sorry, Mom," I stammered. "I didn't mean what I said."

Her fingers banged the keys into a startled crescendo.

"I'm *so* sorry, Mom," I repeated.

She pushed herself up from the piano stool and opened her arms wide. I ran into them. I wanted the embrace to go on forever, but just then the doorbell rang. Molly was waiting for me on the doorstep.

"Perfect! This is the outfit you should wear," Molly said. "I like it even better than your new dress." She was sitting cross-legged on my bed, surrounded by the contents of my closet. I had tried on and discarded every garment I owned. Now I posed in front of my dresser mirror in a navy blue dress with a sailor collar. Even though it hadn't been my first choice, I had to admit that I looked nice in it.

With a knock on the door, Mom came into the room. "What happened here – a hurricane hit your room?" she asked.

"I'll clean up first thing tomorrow morning, I promise! How do I look?"

"Beautiful, darling," she said. "But you must hurry up. Dad says you'll be late if you don't leave right away." She turned to Molly. "They'll drop you at home first."

Dad drove off as I climbed the steps to Jacob's apartment with a box of Laura Secord chocolates clutched in my hands. I paused for a moment to catch my breath and looked around. There was no nameplate on the door, but a small metal cylinder had been affixed to the doorpost. I forgot all about it when the door swung open on the first ring. Jacob's smile widened as his eyes swept over me.

"You look nice!" he said as he helped me off with my jacket. "Everybody wants to meet you." He led me into a small living room full of comfortable worn furniture, soft lighting, and lots of books on shelves.

"This is Alexandra Gal," Jacob announced awkwardly. "These are my parents, Alex," he said, pointing to a middle-aged couple on the sofa. "And this is my sister, Marnie." He nodded at a freckle-faced girl perched in an armchair, and she stuck out her tongue.

Jacob's mother rose from her seat. "Welcome, dear," she said with a smile. "You're the first friend Jacob has brought home since we moved here."

"Nice to meet you," I replied.

"Hi, Alex," said Mr. Pearlman, a large, rumpled man with a pipe. "You're just in time for dinner."

We crowded around the dining-room table, which had been set with cream-colored melamine dishes. Two tall tapers in heavy silver candlesticks burned in the center. Mrs. Pearlman noticed that I was looking at them and said, "They were my mother's. They've been in our family for a long time."

"They're beautiful."

"Thank you. They mean a lot to me."

"They remind me of our candlesticks. Mom told me that they belonged to my grandmother."

"Isn't that nice," she said as she motioned me toward the chair beside Jacob.

"That's my chair!" Marnie cried.

"Not tonight, pumpkin," Mr. Pearlman said. "Let Alex sit beside Jacob. Come, sit next to me."

"But I always –" She broke off mid-sentence at a stern look from her mother and threw herself down on the chair beside her father. "Jake has a girlfriend . . . Jake has a girlfriend," she muttered under her breath.

Jacob's face turned crimson. "Why, I'll –"

"Enough, Jacob!" Mrs. Pearlman said. "Marnie, do you want to spend Shabbos in your room?"

The girl gave the table leg a swift kick but kept quiet. Satisfied, Mrs. Pearlman turned away to cover her head with a silk scarf. Jacob and his father put on black skullcaps, then Mr. Pearlman poured a glass of red wine into a small silver cup and pronounced a few sentences in a language I couldn't understand. He passed the cup around the table, and we all drank from it. Next, he said a few more sentences in the same language over a braided loaf of bread that sat in front of him on the table. He broke off several small pieces, dipped them in salt, and passed a piece to each person around the table. I noticed that everybody was eating their bread, so I ate my piece too. When all of us had finished, Mrs. Pearlman stood up.

"I'll bring in dinner," she said.

"Let me help you," I said.

"Thank you, dear. Marnie will help too."

The table was soon overflowing with bowls and platters. Chicken soup and salad were followed by something Mrs. Pearlman called brisket, which turned out to be the same kind of roast Mom made. We ate potato knishes, homemade pickles, and even a fancy green-bean casserole with onion rings arranged on top. For dessert we had dry cookies that were delicious. Mrs. Pearlman called them komish. We ate and ate until I was so stuffed that I couldn't have eaten another mouthful. Finally, Mr. Pearlman leaned back in his chair.

"It's so nice to have our family together to welcome Shabbos," he said. "And it's also nice to have a guest joining us in our new home. Do you live far from here, Alex?"

"Five minutes away, on Ash Street."

"Jacob tells me that you're in some of his classes," he said.

I nodded. "Social studies and music."

"We've been told that your school is the best high school in the city," he said.

"My school too, Daddy?"

"Yes, Marnie. Your school is very good too." He poured himself a glass of wine before turning back to me. "We're fortunate that our apartment is so close by. It's important to us that Jacob attend a school with such a good reputation."

"You mean it's important to you, Nathan," Mrs. Pearlman said. She shot her husband a quick glance, then turned to me. "Are there many Jewish kids in your school, Alexandra?"

I had to think for a moment before answering, for I had never considered it before. "I guess not. Most of the Jewish people live in the North End, and their kids go to school there. Even the Jewish kids who live around here go to the parochial school in the North End."

"I told you it doesn't matter, Mother!" Jacob cried. "Why do you have to keep harping on the subject?" He cracked his knuckles. I was learning that this meant he was nervous.

"It matters to me," Mrs. Pearlman said. "Marnie is too young, but you should join the B'Nai B'rith Youth Organization as soon as possible. I'm sure they're active in this town too."

"They are," I said. "Last year, my Sunday school class had a bowling team. We bowled against several BBYO teams at the annual city-wide roll-off. They were pretty good."

"I like bowling," Jacob said. "We should go sometime."

Mrs. Pearlman stared at me solemnly. I noticed that her smile had slipped. "So you go to Sunday school," she said. "When you mentioned your grandmother's candlesticks, I was quite certain that you were . . ." Her voice trailed off.

"Mother, stop it!" Jacob cried.

She shrugged her shoulders. "Fine," she said before turning back to me. "Which church does your family belong to?" she asked.

"St. Stephen's Catholic. I go to Sunday school there every week."

"I see. Your last name is Gal. Very unusual. Where's your family from?"

"They came from Hungary before I was born."

She frowned. "Ah, I didn't realize you were greeners."

"Greeners?"

"Immigrants, dear."

Jacob jumped up from the table. "We've got to leave or we'll be late," he said.

His father checked his watch. "We've got lots of time, but I'll take you now if you want."

As we left, both Jacob and his father kissed the tips of their fingers and then touched the metal cylinder on the doorpost. Jacob saw me looking at him.

"It's a mezuzah," he explained. "Most Jewish homes have one. We always kiss it. It's supposed to protect our home."

Fifteen minutes later we were entering the school gym, decorated for the night to resemble a cabaret more than the hall of sweat I was used to. Balloons of different colors and sizes were hanging from the ceiling, and a rainbow of crepe-paper streamers festooned the gray walls. A long table had been set up in a corner. It held bottles of Coca-Cola and bags of potato chips, the student council's fund-raising project. A professional

DJ sat with his collection of rock 'n' roll records and amplifiers by the opposite wall. A pretty woman in a green dress, her hair gathered in loose curls on top of her head, approached us on the arm of a man in a gray suit. It took me a minute to recognize Miss Wilton and Mr. Bradford, our chaperones for the night, in their civilian clothes.

"Time to have fun! Time to dance!" boomed Mr. Bradford.

"You look very pretty, Alexandra," said Miss Wilton.

"Thank you, Miss Wilton. So do you."

As we walked over to the refreshment table, Jacob and I passed Christie Sutherland and her clique of the popular kids in our grade. I smiled at her, but she turned her back on me.

"What a snob," Jacob said.

"She was friendlier at Guides. I don't know what's bothering her."

"Forget about her," Jacob said as he pulled me onto the dance floor.

Only a few couples were dancing. Most of the kids were standing by the wall – the boys on one side of the room, the girls on the other. Molly and Jean were jiving with each other. Molly waved to me, but Jean seemed to be lost in a world of her own, staring into space and not meeting my eyes. I moved a little closer to Jacob and rested my head on his shoulder. Everybody can see that he is my boyfriend, my heart sang.

We didn't leave the dance floor except to buy a bottle of Coke. At ten o'clock, Miss Wilton announced the last dance of the evening. The lights were turned lower and Elvis's romantic voice crooned "Love Me Tender." Jacob pulled me even closer to him. I put my arms around his neck and followed his lead, our steps a perfect match. Both of us were lost in a sea of movement, of music, of feelings.

"Alex," Jacob whispered, "I like you. I really like you a lot."

"I like you too," I said.

Chapter 9

I was in my room sweating over the math problems Miss Wilton had assigned for homework when Dad called up from the bottom of the stairs.

"Alexandra! A phone call for you."

"Who is it?"

"I don't know. A boy," he said.

I bounced down the steps two at a time.

"Careful! Watch where you're going."

I took the receiver and turned my back on him. He took the hint and went into the living room. I closed the door of the foyer before settling down on the bottom step.

"Hi," Jacob said. "It's me."

A long silence. I searched my brain for a clever comment, but nothing came to mind.

"I'm calling to tell you that I had a good time at the dance the other night," he said.

"So did I." Another pause. I seemed to have forgotten all the small talk I'd ever known. "I have a lot of homework," I finally managed to croak.

"Me too," Jacob said. "I guess I'll let you get back to it. I don't want to keep you."

"No, no! I *want* to talk to you."

Relieved laughter on the other end of the line. "That's good. I was beginning to wonder." Jacob laughed again. "Alex, would you like to come to the movies with me next Sunday? G.I. *Blues* is playing at the Odeon. It's supposed to be good."

I clutched the phone to my chest and did a silent dance. A date! A date! He was actually asking me for a real date.

"Alex? Are you still there? If you don't want to come, that's okay too." He sounded disappointed.

"I'd *love* to come. I heard it's a fantastic movie. Elvis is my favorite star." Seeing the picture with Jacob would mean breaking my plans to see it with Jean and Molly, but I knew they would understand.

A sigh of relief blew through the phone lines. "That's

settled, then. Let's go to the matinee. I'll pick you up. If we take the bus, our fathers won't have to drive us."

"Okay, but I'll meet you at the Odeon." That way I won't have to introduce you to Mom and Dad, I thought.

"Are you sure? I don't mind coming to get you."

"It's easier to meet you."

"Okay. I'll phone you on Saturday to let you know what time. Bye for now." With a click, he was gone.

I went into the living room to face my parents. They were on the couch, watching some comedians on Ed Sullivan.

Mom moved closer to Dad to make room on the sofa for me. I sat down beside her.

"Who was that on the phone?" Dad asked. "You know I don't like you to interrupt your homework with phone calls."

"It was Jacob Pearlman. He asked me to the movies next Sunday." It all came out in a rush.

"You can't go," Mom said instantly.

"Why not? I already went to the dance with him."

"You're too young to be alone with a boy."

"Your mother is right," Dad said. "You're not going on a date at your age."

"I'm almost fourteen!"

"It's out of the question."

Mom was silent, her face pale.

"Mom," I beseeched her. "I'm not a baby. Please let me go!"

"It's not only that you're young. The boy is . . ."

"Is what?"

No answer from her.

I took a deep breath to get my voice under control and turned to Dad again. Forcing myself to speak quietly, I said, "It's not like we're going out at night. We're going to the matinee. Please, please let me go."

"Haven't we made our feelings clear?" Dad asked, his voice rising in frustration. "It's useless to talk about it any more. You're *not* going. End of discussion."

I turned to Mom once more. "Please, Mom. Let me go."

She didn't look at me. "You heard your father."

I jumped up from the couch and rushed to the door. "I *will* go out with him! You can't stop me!" I cried, slamming the door behind me as loudly as possible.

The uniformed usher led us to our seats at the Odeon Theater. I sat down and took the tub of popcorn out of Jacob's hand before he slid into the seat next to mine. A moment of awkward silence followed. I took a handful of popcorn.

"So is your family settling in?" I finally asked. "Do they like it here?"

"Dad says that business is good, and Marnie has made

some friends. Mom had a tougher time at first, but she joined Hadassah to meet people. She's never home now." He sighed. "She makes me so mad sometimes. She keeps complaining that we didn't buy a house in the North End. She nagged me so much that I joined the BBYO bowling league."

I took another handful of popcorn. "You're lucky your mother likes to go out. My mother hasn't got any friends, and she never goes anywhere by herself. One of us always has to go with her. It's hard for her. She was in a bad car accident in the old country and almost died from it. There's a large scar on her arm and one on her leg that never healed properly." Changing subjects, I asked, "What about you? Do you like it here?"

He shrugged. "The kids at school aren't very friendly. The boys in my bowling league are much nicer."

I cleared my throat. "Um, what about me?"

He smiled. "And you too, of course, Alex."

"I wouldn't worry. You'll make friends soon enough. It just takes time."

"I hope you're right."

There was a brief commotion, and then the manager of the Odeon appeared on the narrow stage in front of the tall crimson curtains covering the screen.

"May I have your attention, please," he cried. The noisy audience fell silent. "It's time for our weekly draw.

Ten lucky kids will get free Eskimo bars. Get your ticket stubs ready!"

Jacob fished our tickets out of his pocket. "Here, you hold them," he said.

The manager reached into his box. "The first lucky number is 19122001," he announced.

It matched the number of one of our tickets. I waved my hands in the air. "We won! We won! Go get it," I said to Jacob.

"No, you go." He nudged my arm to lever me out of my seat. "Go, before he gives it to somebody else."

I made my way to the front of the theater to the sound of loud clapping from Molly and Jean, who were sitting a few rows ahead of us.

"Remember the ice cream at the beach?" Jacob asked when I got back to my seat. "You almost dropped your cones when those stupid kids threw the ball at you."

"It's a good thing you caught it," I said, smiling at him. "Today, you get to eat the ice cream. You paid for the tickets."

"Don't be silly, Alex. I want you to have it."

"Okay, let's share. I'll break it in half."

"Let me cut it in half. Breaking it will make a mess." He took a Swiss Army knife from his pocket and sliced the bar down the middle. "I got this knife for my bar mitzvah," he explained. "I knew it would come in handy someday."

Just then, the house lights dimmed, the curtains opened, and the Road Runner appeared on the screen. Jacob's hand snuck into my lap and grasped my free hand. I glanced at him in the semi-darkness and saw that he was smiling at me. I smiled back. The next two hours passed by like two fleeting minutes. I was aware of only the warmth of Jacob's shoulder pressing against mine, his closeness, the pressure of his fingers entwined with mine. When the house lights came on at the end of the movie, it was a rude shock.

"Time to go home," Jacob said. He checked his watch. "If we hurry, we'll catch the five o'clock bus. I'll take you home."

"You don't have to."

"I want to. And your parents will be mad if I don't see you to your door."

"They're not home. They usually go for a drive on Sunday afternoons."

With some luck, I'll get home before them, I said to myself, and they'll never find out that I went out with Jacob. I had told them I'd be window shopping with Molly and Jean.

"That's all right," Jacob said. "I still want to take you home."

The bus was clattering to a stop at the street corner just as we got there. A large group of kids elbowed their way up the steps ahead of us. We dropped our tickets into the receptacle and settled into two empty seats. The driver closed the folding doors and was just revving up the motor when through the window I saw Molly and Jean dashing out of the Odeon in our direction.

"Wait! Wait!" I cried. "My friends are coming."

The driver opened the doors again to let them in. Gasping for breath, the girls threw themselves down on seats next to ours.

"I thought we'd missed the bus for sure," Molly said. "The next one doesn't come for another hour."

"Alex told the driver to wait for you," Jacob said.

"Thanks a million!" Molly beamed at me. "How did you guys like the movie? I loved it! Isn't Elvis the cutest guy you ever saw? I guess you wouldn't think so, Alex – *not now*," she said, looking at Jacob and speaking at shotgun speed, as usual.

Through all this, Jean sat silently peering out of the window, her legs primly crossed, her hands clasped in her lap.

"What about you, Jean?" Jacob asked. "Did you like the movie?"

"It was okay," she mumbled, keeping her gaze fixed on the street outside.

"What's the matter with you?" Molly said.

"Nothing." She shrugged but wouldn't look in our direction. Molly rolled her eyes behind her back.

"Your friend Jean doesn't like me," Jacob said as we walked down my street from the bus stop.

"Sure she does. It can't have anything to do with you. I'll talk to her tomorrow and find out what's wrong. She's one of my best friends. She'll tell me what's bothering her."

We walked up the steps to the porch.

"As long as you like me, I don't care what anybody else thinks," Jacob said.

He was standing close to me, smiling, his breath fanning my cheeks. As I looked up at him to return his smile, his head lowered and our lips met. At that very instant, the front door swung open. I pulled away with a gasp.

"Get in the house, Alexandra! At once!" Mom cried. Without another word, she was gone, the door slamming behind her with a loud bang.

"Let me talk to her and explain," Jacob said.

"No, you'd better go. I'll speak to her myself. I'm sorry, but she's been behaving strangely lately."

I watched him turn the corner before I went into the house. Mom was washing dishes at the sink, her back to me. "How dare you disobey us," she said without turning around.

"I don't care what you think," I answered. "We weren't doing anything wrong!"

She finally turned to face me. Two deep lines etched the corners of her mouth and made her look much older than her years. "You will not see that boy again," she said simply before turning back to her dishes.

Anger loosened my tongue. "You can't stop me!" I shouted. "I won't let you!"

She didn't turn around, did not respond, just kept on washing the dishes.

Chapter 10

❀❀❀❀❀❀❀❀❀❀❀❀❀❀❀❀❀❀❀❀❀❀❀❀❀❀

I stayed in my room for the rest of the day. When Mom called up that dinner was ready, I yelled back that I wasn't hungry. I was sorry later on, though; the three pieces of gum that I found in my pocket didn't stop my stomach from grumbling. I was so hungry that I had trouble falling asleep.

I woke up early the next morning, and the smell of breakfast drew me downstairs like a magnet. Mom was standing by the stove in the quilted gold robe that Dad and I had given her for her birthday. She heaped food on my plate and sat down beside me at the kitchen table but did not speak. When I stole a glance at her profile, she seemed absorbed in puffing on one of her interminable cigarettes. I knew I had to tell her how I felt.

"I'm sorry, Mom. I shouldn't have snuck out behind your back."

She flicked her cigarette ash into a crystal ashtray and turned to me. "You *should* be sorry, Alexandra. I'm very surprised at your behavior. I thought I could trust you."

"You can, Mom. You can. But you and Dad weren't fair to me. I just wanted to go to a matinee with Jacob. We weren't doing anything wrong."

She inhaled deeply before speaking. Her hand was shaking so much that the cigarette wobbled. "You must let your father and me judge what's appropriate for you," she finally said.

"Even if you're wrong?"

She sighed and took hold of my hand. "Listen, dear, I know what I'm doing. I know what's best for you. Promise me that you won't go out with this boy again."

"I do promise that I won't sneak around behind your back ever again. But I can't promise not to see Jacob, Mom. I like him. And anyway, you don't even know him."

The doorbell rang. "That must be Olga. I'll let her in." She stood up and hobbled to the door. "We'll finish this conversation another time," she said. "Put a couple of slices of bread into the toaster, please."

She was back a minute later with our Ukrainian cleaning lady hot on her heels. Olga had been coming to our house for as long as I could remember. The woman's round face brightened when she saw me.

As Mom made her way to the counter, the toast popped up with a loud ping. She spread butter and homemade strawberry jam on it, then handed a slice to me.

"Would you like a piece of toast, Olga?" Mom asked.

"Don't mind if I do," Olga said, sitting down beside me.

Before she joined us at the table, Mom poured steaming hot cocoa into my mug and filled her own cup and Olga's with rich, black espresso.

"Good strong coffee," Olga said. "It wakes you up. Not like weak coffee my Canadian ladies make."

Olga had immigrated to Canada the same time as my parents did. She made her living cleaning houses in our neighborhood.

"How many ladies do you clean for, Olga?" I asked.

Olga took a sip of her coffee before answering. "I busy," she finally said. "I have four ladies. They like me."

"I'm not surprised. We like you too, Olga," Mom said.

"Thank you. Mrs. Wallace on Queenston Street, she ask if I work for her new neighbor, Mrs. Pearlman."

"I know the Pearlmans," I said. "Their son, Jacob, is my friend."

Olga frowned. "I refuse job at their house."

"I guess you don't want to work every day," Mom said.

"It's not that. I need money. But Mrs. Wallace tell me Mrs. Pearlman is Jew. I Christian woman. I don't work for kikes."

"What are kikes?" I asked.

"Hush," said Mom. The blood drained out of her face. "I never want to hear you using such language!"

Olga scratched her head. "What you mean, Mrs. Gal? You think Christian woman should work for kikes?"

Mom stood up so quickly that her cane fell to the floor with a loud clatter. I picked it up and handed it to her. She grasped its handle so tightly that her knuckles turned white. "I'm sorry, Olga. I won't be needing you today after all," she said in a quiet voice.

The cleaning women stared at her, her mouth wide open. "What is matter, Mrs. Gal? I always come to you on Mondays."

"Not today, I'm afraid." She made her way over to the drawer where she kept her shopping money and pulled out a handful of cash. She shoved it into the pocket of Olga's apron. "This should cover what you would have earned here today." Suddenly, she seemed to notice that I was still there. "Alexandra," she said, "please leave for school immediately."

"I don't have to. It's still early."

"Do what I say!"

She was using her "I will be obeyed" voice, so I did as I was told without any further argument.

When I got home in the afternoon, there was no sign of the cleaning woman.

"What happened with Olga?" I asked.

"She's gone," Mom said, a stern expression on her face. "She won't be coming back."

"You *fired* her? But she's been working for us for as long as I can remember!"

She cut off my words with a wave of her hand. "Never mind," she said simply, then she walked to the door and closed it quietly behind her.

Chapter 11

🌿🌿🌿🌿🌿🌿🌿🌿🌿🌿🌿🌿🌿🌿🌿🌿🌿🌿🌿🌿🌿🌿🌿🌿

The Saturday morning sun streamed through the kitchen window and warmed our faces. Mom and I had arranged Tupperware bowls and wooden spoons on the kitchen counter. Now we were measuring out the ingredients my friends and I would need for our baking session. I put a dozen eggs into a glass bowl and placed a slab of butter on a wooden chopping board.

"Could you please check if the mail has arrived?" Mom asked as she dipped a measuring cup into a large brown flour canister decorated with daisies.

I took the key off a hook by the door and went to open the mailbox. There was only one envelope, a thin one with Mom's name written on it in a spidery handwriting.

It was addressed to 39 Ash Street. Our house number was 43. I turned it over. It was from somebody called Judit Weltner.

By the time I got back to the kitchen, Mom had poured flour into one of the bowls. She'd also taken a cookie sheet and a couple of baking pans out of the cabinets.

"Everything's ready," she announced. She saw the envelope in my hand. "So who is writing us?"

"Somebody called Judit Weltner. Who is she, Mom? I've never heard you mention her."

She grabbed the envelope out of my hand. "Impossible!" she cried. "Jutka is dead!" She tried to tear the envelope open, but her hands were shaking so badly that she couldn't loosen the flap.

"Let me help you," I offered.

"I'll do it myself!" she said, taking out a pair of large scissors and cutting the envelope open. She sank down on a chair and pulled out a sheet of paper that was filled with the same spidery writing I'd noticed on the envelope. She scanned the page anxiously. "She's alive. Thank God!" she cried, her voice full of joy. But suddenly, all the color ran out of her face. "No, no! She mustn't come here. She mustn't!" She broke off and bit her lip, as if to stop herself from saying more.

I peered over her shoulder and tried to read the letter. "What does she say, Mom? What language is she using?"

"Hungarian. I —" Just then, the doorbell rang. She folded up the letter and shoved it into her pocket. "Please answer the door," she said. "Your friends have arrived."

By the time I'd led Jean and Molly into the kitchen, Mom wore her usual serene expression. Nobody could have guessed that anything had upset her as she went from girl to girl to supervise what we were doing. Before long, I was mixing the ingredients for a cheesecake while Molly was stirring the batter for a batch of chocolate chip cookies. Jean was the most ambitious of all of us. Mom was showing her how to stretch out the thin dough for a strudel.

"Don't be afraid that the dough will have holes in it. The thinner you can get it, the better your strudel will turn out," she explained.

Jean followed her instructions, her face scrunched up in concentration. "My dough looks perfect," she finally crowed.

Mom then showed her how to use a pastry brush to paint egg white onto the dough. "All that's left is to fill it with apples and walnuts and raisins," she said. "You can do that by yourself."

"I wish my mother was as much fun as yours," Jean said after Mom had left the kitchen.

"She isn't always like this, believe me. Sometimes she drives me crazy."

I concentrated for the next few minutes on mixing my batter. I had so much to tell my friends that I didn't know where to start. I wanted to tell them about Mom's reaction to the photos we'd found. I also wanted to tell them that she disliked Jacob, even though she'd never met him, and that I was running out of excuses to stop him from coming over to my house. There was so much I wanted to say, but the memory of the misery on Mom's face when I'd questioned her about the photos stopped me from speaking. I settled for telling them what Mrs. Cowan had said to Jacob at the yard sale and describing how upset he'd been.

"Poor Jacob," Molly said. "I never thought about the meaning of the term 'jew me down.'"

"Me neither."

"I don't blame him for being insulted," she added.

Jean was silent.

I kept stirring the gooey mixture in the bowl on the counter. It was somehow easier to talk if I didn't have to look right at them. "I wonder if I should quit Guides. I don't want Mrs. Cowan for a captain."

"Alex, no!" Molly cried. "You've been wanting to join for years."

Jean put the pastry brush on the kitchen counter and faced me. "I don't see why you're blaming Mrs. Cowan," she said. "She couldn't have known that Jacob would be so touchy."

I couldn't believe what I was hearing. "Touchy? How can you say that? She's a grown-up. She should know what she's saying," I cried. "You would have felt just like Jacob, Jean."

"Come on, Jean," Molly said. "You don't mean that."

Jean shrugged, picked up a spatula, and became engrossed, once again, in the pastry in front of her. Molly and I just stared at her. Finally, Molly broke the silence.

"What's wrong with you, Jean? You didn't mean that, did you?" she repeated.

"I guess not," Jean mumbled.

I knew that somehow I had to ease the tension in the room. "Let's talk about something else," I said in a determinedly cheerful voice. "Do you want to go to the movies tonight?"

"What do you mean?" Molly said. "Did you forget that it's Christie Sutherland's party tonight? What are you going to wear?"

"I told you she didn't invite me." I looked from Molly to Jean and back again. "You said you weren't going either."

Molly stared at me with a crestfallen expression. "She came up to Jean and me after school yesterday and asked us to come. I took it for granted that she'd asked you too."

"Well, she didn't, but I couldn't care less." I spoke in a casual voice, although I would have given anything to go to Christie's party. All the popular kids would be there. "She's probably jealous that I have a boyfriend."

"That's no reason for her to act like that," Molly said. "It's a mean thing to do. Well, if you're not going, we won't either. Right, Jean?"

Jean didn't reply. She just kept on spreading the apple filling, her face impassive.

"What's wrong with you, Jean?" Molly asked. "Why aren't you talking to us?"

Jean balanced the edge of her spatula on the rim of a plate before speaking. "Well," she finally said, turning to me, "you can't expect Christie to invite you if you're going out with Jacob."

"Why?"

She shrugged her shoulders. "I don't know," she said. "No reason, I guess." She turned to Molly. "I think you and I should go to the party, though. It would hurt Christie's feelings if we didn't show up."

"And what about Alex's feelings? If she doesn't go, I don't want to either!" Molly declared. "I'm surprised at you, Jean. Everybody calls us the Three Musketeers. We do everything together."

"Don't be so childish," Jean said. "I'm going, and I'm sure Alex doesn't care."

"Of course you should go," I said. I hoped the fake smile on my face wouldn't let her guess how much she was hurting me. "You should go too, Molly."

"No way!" Molly caught Jean's sleeve. "What's wrong with you? Why are you being so weird?"

Jean pulled away. "I'm not!" she said. "It's just that . . . Oh, never mind." She threw down her spatula. "I have to leave now," she announced. "I have to go somewhere with my mother. Alex, could you please put my strudel into the oven at 350 degrees for half an hour? I'll come by tomorrow to pick it up, if that's all right."

"Okay, but –"

"I've got to run now," she said. "See you tomorrow."

Before I could reply, she had disappeared.

"What's the matter with her?" Molly asked. She sat down heavily on a kitchen chair. "Sometimes I feel as if I don't know her at all."

"Me neither. She's certainly been acting strangely. Jacob thinks she doesn't like him. Do you remember how unfriendly she was to him on the bus?"

"I do. After you got off, I asked her why she was like that to him. She wouldn't tell me."

"Well, it's no use asking her again. You know how stubborn she is. She'll tell us when she's ready."

Mom came into the kitchen. "Dr. Gal has to make a housecall, Molly. He can drop you off at your house, if you'd like." She looked around the room. "Where's Jean?"

"She had to leave early, Mom."

"That's too bad. Dad could have taken her home too."

"I'll get my jacket, Mrs. Gal," Molly said as they left the kitchen.

Chapter 12

❋❋❋❋❋❋❋❋❋❋❋❋❋❋❋❋❋❋❋❋❋❋❋❋❋❋❋❋❋❋

When Dad came home, I told him about the mystery letter. He said nothing. Instead, he went straight upstairs to see Mom. I could hear their voices, but I couldn't make out what they were saying.

When he finally came back downstairs, Dad said, "The letter you were asking about is from an old friend of your mother's. It's nothing for you to worry about." Then he went into the den and shut the door behind him.

I spent the rest of the afternoon watching an old movie on TV, but I barely followed it. I kept thinking about how much I wanted to call Jean to find out why she disliked Jacob. As if it had a mind of its own, my hand reached for the telephone. But as I was dialing her number, I realized that she would be getting ready for Christie's party. Despite what I had said, I was still terribly hurt that she wanted to go without me. I slammed the receiver back onto the cradle just as Mom and Dad came into the room. Mom was a little more pale than usual, but she looked smart in a blue wool dress and a matching hat with a feather in it. Her coat was draped over her arm. Dad was wearing his black suit. I started to ask them about the letter, but a look from Dad stopped me.

"Well, we're ready to head off to the Glenn Gould concert. When I hear his music, I forget everything," Mom said in a wistful tone.

One look at my face was enough for her to know that something was wrong. "What's the matter?" she asked. "Are you feeling sick? You're a little pale." She felt my forehead. "You don't feel warm, but why don't you lie down? You may be coming down with something." She took off her hat and put down her coat on the sofa. "I'll stay home with you."

"No, Mom. I'm okay. I have a little headache, that's all. Please go! I know how much you love the music."

"I can't leave you alone when you may be sick, dear. You go without me, Jonah."

"I will not!" Dad said. "You're coming with me, Agi. You need to get out of the house."

"But I'm worried about Alexandra being –"

Dad interrupted her. "It'll do you good to go to the concert."

"It's just that –"

He patted her hand. "Don't worry about Alexandra. There's nothing wrong with her, and we'll be home in a couple of hours anyway. She'll take an aspirin and her headache will be gone by the time we return."

"Dad's right, Mom. Please go. I'll be fine."

It took us several minutes to convince her to leave. I breathed a sigh of relief when the front door finally clicked closed behind them. I turned on the TV again but still couldn't concentrate, so I began to wander the house aimlessly. I suddenly realized that this was my big chance to look again at the photographs hidden in Mom's drawer. I was especially curious about the girl who looked like me.

Without any more delay, I raced to my parents' bedroom and pulled out the bottom drawer of Mom's dresser, careful not to displace the scarves in it. I reached under the green scarf on top, but this time my fingers did not touch the flat package. Mom must have moved it, I thought. I took out all the scarves and unfolded them – still no photos. Then I rifled through the rest of the drawers. Hidden below the lace mantilla Mom wore to church was the letter that had come that morning. But the photographs were nowhere to be found.

I turned my attention to Dad's tall chest of drawers. The photographs weren't there either. By then, I was flinging piles of my parents' clothing onto the floor. I peered at the top and bottom of the closet. I crouched down and checked under the bed. I even lifted the mattress and slipped my hand underneath it. No sign of the photos.

I checked my watch. Over an hour had passed since Mom and Dad had gone out. It was time to start folding the clothing I had flung about and putting it back in place. I was just returning the last pair of socks to a drawer when the doorbell startled me. I looked at my watch again. It was still too early for Mom and Dad to have returned.

I peeked through the spy hole in the front door and saw a small woman with brown hair in an elegant black overcoat. She held a small suitcase in her hand. She seemed harmless enough and there was even something familiar about her, so I swung the door open. When she saw me, she took a step forward, her arms stretched wide.

"Agi," she cried, continuing on in what sounded like Hungarian.

I stepped back. "I'm sorry, but I can't understand you. My name is Alexandra. My mother's name is Agi. What can I do for you?"

"Yes, of course. Alexandra, like your grandmother of blessed memory," the woman replied in a soft voice with an accent that sounded like Mom's. "I am being silly. Of course you wouldn't speak Hungarian." She enunciated her words carefully, the way people sometimes do when their first language is not English. "I'm sorry if I frightened you. I had forgotten for a moment that the years have passed. When I last saw your dear mother, more than fifteen years ago, she looked the way you do today."

"Everybody says that I look like Mom. Did you come to see her? She isn't home."

"I am Jutka!"

She looked at me as if she expected me to know who she was. Her name was familiar, but I couldn't remember where I had heard it before, so I shook my head.

"Your mother hasn't talked about me?" she asked, her voice laced with disappointment. Suddenly, she glanced at the doorframe, her features clouded with confusion. "Where is the mezu –" She broke off and leaned against the door. "Please, may I come in and wait for your mother? I'm so tired. I traveled through the night to get here."

I knew I wasn't supposed to invite strangers into the house, but she looked so exhausted that I couldn't bear to leave her standing outside. I'm bigger than she is, I told myself, so she won't be able to hurt me. "Please, come in," I found myself saying, and I led her into the living room.

"What a lovely home you have," she said. "Agi always loved beautiful things. So did your grandmama." She walked up to the piano. "Do you play?"

"A little. I used to take lessons, but I wasn't very good. Mom's the real musician in the family."

"Your mother and I had the same teacher a million years ago. Do you mind if I . . . ?" she asked, pointing to the piano. "I can never resist."

"Go ahead. I love music."

Her eyes closed and her fingers flew over the keyboard like the wings of a butterfly, coaxing notes from the belly of the black beast. The music reminded me of roaring waves in a stormy sea. Then the waves flattened, becoming gentle and soft until they gradually dissipated. Her hands rested lightly on the keys for a final stretched-out note before she turned to me.

I was at a loss for words. "You're a wonderful pianist," I finally said.

"I used to be. Never as good as your mama, of course. Both of us dreamt of the concert stage, but that was before . . ."

"Before what?"

She didn't reply. She seemed to be staring at the cross around my neck, just as Mr. McCallum had done that day in the church.

"What's the matter?" I asked. "Why are you looking at my necklace?"

"Oh, it's nothing. Nothing at all."

She closed the piano and picked up one of the three photographs displayed on top. The first was my school picture, the second a stiffly posed family photo. The one she was looking at was a snapshot that Dad had taken of Mom that summer at the beach. She was sitting on a bench beside the lake, her face lifted toward the sun as if she was trying to absorb all of its warmth.

I was suddenly reminded of another picture I had seen – the photograph of the four women in the garden. There was something about this woman's expression that made me look at her more closely. She was the girl with the dark hair in the photographs I'd found, I realized. And her name – Jutka – wasn't that one of the names on the back of one of the photographs? Wasn't it also the name Mom had called out when she read the mysterious letter for the first time?

"You're the girl in Mom's photographs, aren't you?" I cried. "You also wrote her a letter, didn't you? Who are you? What are you doing here?"

"I don't understand. I know nothing about any photographs," she said. "Your dear mama is my oldest friend. I did write her a letter, but she never answered me." She kissed Mom's picture and said, "My beloved Agi."

"What are you doing? Who are you?" I repeated. She seemed so emotional that I began to feel a bit panicked. What if she didn't know Mom at all, I suddenly thought, and was just some crazed woman I'd let into our home? I moved closer to the fireplace, within reach of the bellows resting by the hearth. I could use it to defend myself if she turned violent.

"Please! Please! You have nothing to fear from me," she said, noticing the alarm on my face. "Agi and I have been friends ever since we were girls. I love her like a sister. She saved my life. She sacrificed herself for me!"

I stared at her, my curiosity at war with my fear.

"Look," she said, rolling up her left sleeve and displaying a series of blue numbers on her forearm. "We even lied about our last names so we could stay together in the camp. Agi's number is A10235. Mine is A10234."

By then I was convinced that I was facing a madwoman. "What are you talking about? My mother doesn't have any numbers tattooed on her arm." I pointed to the door. "Get out!"

"I'm sorry," she said. "I didn't know that –"

She was distracted by the sound of a key turning in the front door. I started breathing easier when I heard my parents' voices. They appeared in the doorway, and Mom's hand flew to her throat at the sight of the stranger. I couldn't read the expression on her face. She shuddered deeply and stretched out her arms toward the woman.

"Jutka! Jutka!" she cried. "It's so good to see you. Until your letter came, I thought you were dead."

The two women engulfed each other in a tight embrace, their tears intermingling. Then it was Dad's turn to be hugged.

"Alexandra," Mom said, "I'm so glad you welcomed my darling Jutka to our home."

"Who is she, Mom?" I asked.

"Explanations can wait," Dad said. "Jutka should have something to eat. We'll talk after the meal." He patted my face. "Well, sweetheart," he said, "it seems that you'll be getting some answers to your questions."

Although it was late, Mom filled the table, and we all sat down to eat. I picked at my food and waited for someone to tell me what was going on.

"Let's speak English," Dad suggested, "so Alexandra can understand."

"Jonah, do you think that's a good idea?" Mom asked.

"Can't you see that the time has come for her to be told the truth?" Dad turned to Jutka and said, "We're surprised to see you. Your letter came only this morning."

"I wrote to you a month ago, as soon as I found out where you lived," she said. "When you didn't reply, I became worried and bought a train ticket so I could come here myself."

"You didn't have the right address," Mom said. "That's why it took so long for your letter to arrive. How did you find our house?"

"Your neighbors next door told me you live here," Jutka said.

"My darling Jutka, I'm so glad that both of us got to Canada! Do you remember how we used to dream about coming here?" Mom asked.

"How could I forget?" Jutka said. "It's a miracle that I'm here. I was taken to another camp when we were separated, and after I was liberated, I spent months in a DP camp. I was sick with typhus for a long time and nearly died. When I finally recovered, I discovered that no one was left. Neither my mama nor my papa had survived. Nor had my brother. My grandmama was also gone. I was an orphan. I thought that you, too, were lost to me, dear Agi. There seemed to be no point in returning home." She wiped her eyes. "Anyway, after a long, long time, I received my papers and immigrated to Canada. I was finally able to turn our childhood dream into a reality."

"My poor dear," Mom said, her own eyes bright with unshed tears.

Agi laughed wryly. "Hold on! My tale of woe becomes even more desperate." The smile on her lips masked the sadness of her eyes. "Once I got here, I quickly realized that the streets of Canada are not paved with gold as we had always thought."

"It must have been very difficult for you," Dad said.

"It was. I was so young, so lonely. But I didn't give up. I went back to school and received my high school diploma. I met a wonderful man whom I love very much. Now I'm enrolled in university." She laughed. "I'm the oldest student in my class, but I'll be graduating in another year." She smiled proudly. "Life is good."

"How did you find us?" I asked.

"Yes, how?" echoed Mom.

"Oh, my dear, it took me a long time. After the war, I wrote to your grandmama's housekeeper. Julia wrote back that both you and Jonah had come back and had married. Finally, news that someone I loved was still alive!" She squeezed Mom's hand. "Julia also told me that you had changed your name from Goldberg to Gal, and that you had immigrated to Canada. But she didn't have your address."

"We wanted to cut all ties with the old country," Mom mumbled. I noticed that she was staring at the table-cloth, not meeting Jutka's eyes.

"All this talking is making me thirsty," Jutka said. She drank from the glass of water in front of her before continuing with her story. "Well, I was desperate to find you. I asked everyone I could think of if they knew where you were. I was able to trace you to Toronto, but then you seemed to have disappeared from the face of the earth.

"Finally, when I was at my doctor's for a checkup, I came up with the idea to write to the medical associations in all the provinces to find out if there was a Dr. Jonah Gal on their rosters. When I received your address, I almost fainted from joy. I wrote you immediately, and when you didn't reply, I decided to book a train ticket and come here myself. And here I am!" she said, breaking into tears once again.

"And I'm so glad!" Mom said, leaning across the table and hugging her.

Then Jutka's tone became serious. "I'm overjoyed to see both you and Jonah again – and to meet your wonderful daughter. It gives me the greatest pleasure." She patted my hand. "So tell me, Jutka, about your life in Canada. You must be doing well, for you have such a lovely home. But there are several things I don't understand. Why is your daughter wearing a cross around her neck? And why don't you have a mezuzah on your doorpost?"

Mom's face paled, and Dad looked grim. Neither of them uttered a word.

"What is Jutka talking about, Mom? Dad?" I asked. "Why shouldn't I wear a cross? And why would we have a mezuzah at the door? Jacob told me that Jewish people have them. Why would *we* have one?"

My parents remained silent.

"I'm sorry," said Jutka at last. "I didn't realize . . . I didn't mean to . . ." She shifted in her chair. "Agi, you must know that I would never intentionally hurt you."

Dad slapped his fist into his palm. "I knew I shouldn't have listened to you, Agi! I knew this would happen! It was a horrendous mistake. I would never have agreed to it if I hadn't had to worry about making a living for my family. Did you actually believe we could live a lie forever? We must tell Alexandra the truth."

Jutka leaned forward and faced Mom. "Tell your daughter our story, Agi. You can't protect her from the truth."

"It seems that I have no choice," Mom said in a resigned tone. "We wanted to protect you," she began, grasping my hands. "We never wanted you to know how much we suffered. It breaks my heart that this is no longer possible. Your father and Jutka are right, however.

You must be told the truth. It will upset you and may even make you weep, but that can't be helped either."

Her words flowed haltingly at first, but then she began to speak with more and more force. "My darling daughter, we are not who you thought we were. We are not Catholic – we are Jewish," she said.

I gaped at her. "What do you mean?"

"You heard me right," she said. "We are Jews, not Catholics. We suffered terribly for our faith. We were imprisoned in concentration camps. The three of us survived, but so many did not. The Nazis murdered our families."

"It was more terrible in the camps than you can imagine." Jutka picked up the story. "They abused us, tattooed us, herded us like cattle. Your dear mother saved my life. When one of the SS guards wanted to shoot me, she threw herself on top of me and took the bullet in her leg in my stead." Her voice cracked with emotion. "I wouldn't be here today without you, Agi!" she said.

Mom held up her hand. "Hush, Jutka. The less said about that, the better it is. I don't want Alexandra to know the horror of it. I vowed to myself in Auschwitz that if by some miracle I survived and had a normal life, I would make sure that no child of mine would suffer like we suffered. I wanted to keep you safe," she said to me. "I didn't want you to know about the wretchedness we endured. I'm certainly not going to tell you about it now."

"But I don't understand," I said. "What kind of camp were you in? And how did you get free if you'd been shot?"

"At the end of the war, when the Soviets came and liberated the few of us who were still alive," she said with a bitter smile, "I was wounded, maimed, almost dead, but free!" She stopped talking for a moment, taking my hands again and grasping them so tightly that she was hurting me.

"Listen to me carefully," she said. "As I lay in the hospital week after week, being nursed back to health, I kept repeating my vow – to keep any future child of mine safe. After I'd recovered, I went back home to look for my family. My story is the same as Jutka's. Not a single person from my family returned. None of them survived the camps – not my mother, not my father, not any of my relatives. Nobody at all! I thought Jutka was dead too. Then, miraculously, your father came home some weeks later!" She smiled, misty eyed, at Dad before turning back to me.

"We were sweethearts before he was deported, and when we saw each other again, we fell in love once more. I was nineteen years old and all alone in the world," she continued, "as was your father, so we decided to marry. But I was still scared. I didn't feel safe in a place where many of our own countrymen wanted us dead. I convinced your father that we should change our name. It used to be Goldberg, but Gal sounds more Hungarian. It didn't help. Our neighbors told us they'd known nothing about the camps. They'd ask, 'Where is your papa? What happened to your dear mama and grand-mama?' I realized then that our future lay elsewhere.

"One day, I noticed that the scarlet-and-gold curtains that had hung in our parlor before the war were blowing in the windows of a house down the street. I knew they were our drapes because they'd been the talk of the town when my mama brought them home after one of her visits to Budapest. I asked for them back, but their new owners denied they were mine. There was nothing I could do.

"When I found out that I was expecting a baby, I begged your father to emigrate. I wanted to leave Hungary. It wasn't my home any more." She kissed my cheek. "I loved you even before you were born, and I wanted a good life for you. Before we were taken away, we'd buried all our money and jewelry in the cellar. But a neighbor had found it. Everything was gone. Your belongings too," she said to Jutka.

"I can't say I'm surprised." She shrugged.

"Fortunately, Julia, our housekeeper – God bless her – had managed to rescue my mama's fur coat, our silver candlesticks, and the precious photographs that you discovered in my dresser. The dear soul returned every-thing to me after the war. I couldn't bear to part with the candlesticks, so I sold Mama's coat to pay for our passage to our new country. That reminds me," she said to Jutka, "I have something that's yours." She grasped hold of her cane and limped out of the room. A minute later, she was back with the book I'd found in her dresser clasped under her arm. She handed it to Jutka. "Aren't you glad you gave it to Julia for safekeeping?" she asked.

"My *Canada* book!" Jutka said, stroking the stained cover with gentle fingers. "I thought it was lost forever."

"Julia returned it to me," Mom said. "When you didn't come home, I couldn't bring myself to leave it behind. It reminded me of you. Open it!"

Jutka burst into tears when she saw the photographs lodged between the cover and the front page of the book. She picked up the picture of the four women.

"My mama and grandmama!" she cried. "I have no pictures of them."

"You do now," Mom said. "I want you to have those." She turned to me. "We weren't allowed to own cameras during the war. If those photographs had ever been dis-covered, we would have faced severe punishment."

She picked up the picture of the girl with the blonde hair who looked like me.

"I was pretty, wasn't I?" she asked, peering closely at

the photo. "It's too bad that my mother was our photographer. I don't have a single picture left of her."

Jutka kissed her on the cheek. "Thank you, my dear. You've given me a priceless gift. But please go on with your story."

"Where was I?" Mom said.

"You sold you mother's fur coat for your passage to Canada," I reminded her. "What happened after that?"

"The hard part was escaping from Hungary. But that's a story for another day. I'll just say for now that we made it out safely, sailed in a large ship across the ocean, and settled in Toronto. You were born there, Alexandra. As I've already told you many times, Dad studied day and night, and he soon learned English and passed his medical exams. Life was good. We joined a synagogue, made friends. Then one day, your father applied for admission privileges at one of the major hospitals. His application was refused. Dad became suspicious when he heard that a doctor with inferior qualifications was approved. A colleague told him that several of the hospitals refused to grant privileges to Jewish physicians. Your father and I were outraged.

"I began to worry that if something like that could happen in Canada, then we weren't any safer here than in Europe. I convinced your father that the only way to make sure that we wouldn't suffer because of who we are was never to reveal the truth to anyone – and that included you. We decided it was safer for you not to know who you are. I even had my tattoo removed," she said, holding out her arm to display the white scar on its underside. "Fortunately, your father was never given a tattoo," she continued. "It took some doing, but I convinced him to go along with my plan. We decided to move here and begin a new life as Christians."

"Against my better judgment," Dad cut in. "I agreed only because I was worried about supporting my family," he repeated. "You heard what Mr. McCallum said in the church that day, Alexandra. My friend Sam Kohn is an excellent doctor, yet he's struggling to make a living. Many patients don't want to go to a Jewish doctor."

"So that's what he was talking about," I said.

"I knew all the deceit would lead to trouble," Dad said. "I told your mother that it's not possible to pack away the past like an old dress in a trunk. I kept wondering if Sam was right and I should have just taken my chances."

I had never heard my father sound so emotional.

He patted my hair. "You must have a lot of questions, Alexandra," he said. "But let's save them for later. Go up to your room and give yourself a chance to think over what your mother has told you. Then we'll talk."

Chapter 13

※※※※※※※※※※※※※※※※※※※※※※※※※※

I sat down on the edge of my bed. I felt like crawling back into it and pulling the covers over my head, but I knew that would solve nothing. I thought of Mom and Dad suffering during the war, of the murder of my grandparents. I thought about how all this had happened because they were Jewish. Not Catholic, like I'd always believed, but Jewish. Did that mean that I was Jewish too? But I felt Catholic! How could I be anything else?

I walked over to my dresser to straighten my hair in the mirror. The girl reflected back at me had my face, my nose, my eyes, my curly hair. She had a mother and a father. She was a ninth-grade student at Lord Selkirk

High, and she attended Sunday school every week at St. Stephen's Catholic Church. There was a boy she liked a lot called Jacob, and he liked her back. The girl in the mirror was me, yet not me. I was the same, but different. I was not who I thought I was. I watched my reflection in the mirror as I mouthed the words "Who are you?"

I pulled the elastic band off my ponytail, brushed my hair, and tied it up neatly. The gold cross at my neck gleamed brightly against my blouse. I traced its outline. The delicate edges were sharp against my fingers. Then I went to bed, hoping that sleep would quickly come.

I was running through a dark forest in a thunderstorm. The gigantic trees surrounding me bent and wept under the lashing of the wind. The only light came from great bolts of lightning in the sky. Each patch of brightness was accompanied by the deafening drumbeat of a celestial symphony. My hands and face were bleeding, scratched to pieces by the bushes that blocked my way and tore my thin dress to shreds. There was a great flash of fire in the sky, and then the vegetation around me burst into flames. Despite the torrential rain, the crackling flames rose up in every direction. Flames blocked the path ahead of me. Flames roared behind me. Flames consumed the trees to my left and the bushes to my right. Even the heavens above burned bright red. Smoke filled my lungs and I began to cough. I stood rooted to the path as the flames came closer and closer, ready to devour my flesh. The sweat on my brow mingled with the rain beating down on my face. I looked around wildly for a means of escape, but there was nowhere to run. Suddenly, somebody was calling my name. I peered into the flames but could not see who it was. Then I woke up.

"Alexandra, wake up! Breakfast is ready," Mom called from downstairs.

I sat up on the edge of my bed and shook my head to rid my brain of its cobwebs. Then I remembered. I remembered what Mom had told me the night before. I shivered and hugged myself.

"Hurry up, lazybones!"

Before heading downstairs, I brushed my teeth, pulled a comb through my hair, and threw on some jeans and an old blouse I rarely wore.

At the kitchen table, my parents and Jutka waited expectantly. Mom smiled nervously when I entered the room.

"So, darling, have you recovered from last night?" she asked in a wavering voice. Then, without waiting for a reply, she said, "Eat your breakfast." She gestured at a tall stack of waffles at the center of the table.

We were all silent as we attacked the food on our plates. I drank deeply from the steaming mug of cocoa that Mom had made for me. I wasn't really hungry, but I forced down every morsel to avoid another argument with her. When I finally leaned back in my chair, I was uncomfortably full.

Dad spoke first. "Now comes the hard part," he said. "Trying to answer your questions."

"We don't have much time to talk," Mom said.

"Why not?" I asked.

"Have you forgotten that we're going to the Ladies' Auxiliary luncheon today? It's at Dr. Wolfe's house this time. I promised Mary Wolfe that I'd be there, and we never –"

"Break a promise." I finished her statement in a sing-song voice.

"What about me?" Jutka asked.

"You're coming with us, of course," Mom said.

"If Jutka is going to be there, do I have to go?" Because only women were allowed at the auxiliary meetings, Dad could not take Mom. I was elected to go in his place, but I found the meetings excruciatingly boring.

A look of panic flitted across her features. It was gone

so quickly that I might have missed it if I didn't know her so well.

"Of course you'll come too," she said, chewing on the cuticle of her left thumb.

"First, we must give Alex the opportunity to talk to us," Dad said. "You still have lots of time."

She shrugged her shoulders. "So what do you want to know, darling?"

"I feel so confused," I told them. "We're Jewish, not Catholic. How could you hide something so important from me?"

Dad patted my arm. "We know this must be a shock for you."

"I'm sorry that my coming here has caused you so much pain," Jutka whispered.

"Don't be silly," Dad said. "I always thought that Alexandra had the right to know the truth."

Mom remained silent.

Dad turned to me. "I know it's a lot to take in at once," he said.

"Why did you have to tell me at all? What will my friends say? None of them is Jewish. I don't even know any Jewish kids except Jacob, and we never talk about our religions!" Once I'd started yelling, I couldn't stop. "It's not fair! You grew up Jewish, but I know nothing about it. Being Catholic is all I know!"

Dad nodded his head. "I realize that," he said. "We haven't been fair to you. We've robbed you of something very important."

Mom leaned over and kissed my cheek. "Forgive me, darling," she said. "I wanted to keep you safe. That's why I didn't tell you about the past. And that's also why I didn't want you to see Jacob. I didn't want your friends, especially a boyfriend, to be Jewish. I wanted to cut all ties with our old lives."

I took a deep breath to calm down before speaking. "We live in Canada," I began. "I feel awful that you suffered so much in the old country, but nobody is going to hurt you here."

Mom shook her head sadly. "What happened to us can happen anywhere. We're safe only if they don't know who we are."

"You're wrong, Mom! It all happened a long time ago, far away, in another country. It has nothing to do with our lives here. It has nothing to do with *me*!"

"Don't try reasoning with your mother on this issue. I've argued with her until I was blue in the face, but I couldn't get her to budge," Dad interjected. I could see by the high color in his face that he was angry. "I'm glad we had to tell you the truth. You're a clever girl, and I know you'll come to understand what we did and why.

For now, ask me anything. I'll try to answer your questions as honestly as I can."

"I don't know what to ask, Dad. I don't even know how Jewish people are different from Christians."

"People are people, Alexandra," he said. "We all worship the same God. But Christians believe in Jesus Christ, while we Jews are still awaiting our Messiah."

"Not believe in Jesus! But, Dad, then you won't be saved!"

He stopped my words with a wave of his hand. "See what we've done," he said to Mom in a harsh voice I'd never heard him use before. He turned back to me with a sad smile. "Why don't you to talk to Father Mike?" he suggested. "He's a decent man. He'll be able to help you."

"No!" Mom cried. "She should tell nobody! No one must know!"

"Mom, I'm almost fourteen years old. You should let me decide for myself. I have to do what's best for me, not what's best for you."

"Alexandra, I'm begging you not to tell anyone," Mom pleaded wildly.

Through all this, Jutka had been silent, her head turning from one parent to the other as they spoke. "Agi," she said now, "by denying who you are, you dishonor the memory of your papa and your mama, of all your relatives who were murdered in Auschwitz for the sake of our religion." She covered her face with her hands. "What happened to you, my Agi? You had the heart of a lion. You saved my life!"

"I just want Alexandra to be safe."

Mom looked so wretched that I wanted to reassure her. "I'll think over everything," I told her. "And I promise that I won't tell anybody before talking to you." I turned back to Dad. "I do have one important question I'd like to ask now, though. Why did the Nazis hate you so? And not just the Nazis but other people too. You should have heard how Mrs. Cowan spoke to Jacob and what Olga said about Jewish people. What do people have against you?"

The silence around the table was fractured by Dad's deep sigh. "My dear daughter, I don't have an answer for you. I wish I did."

The clock on the wall showed that it was nine o'clock. I stood up. "I'd better get ready. Molly will be here soon to pick me up for Sunday school."

"I phoned her mother and told her that you wouldn't be going today," Mom said. "You need time by yourself to think things over."

I looked at her gratefully.

"Enough serious talk for now," Dad said. He walked over to the desk under the window and took a pad of paper and a pencil from a drawer. "Jutka is determined to leave tomorrow. You have the luncheon today, so tomorrow morning is our only chance to show her our city. Let's make a list of all the wonderful places we should take her."

Chapter 14

✳✳✳✳✳✳✳✳✳✳✳✳✳✳✳✳✳✳✳✳✳✳✳✳✳✳✳✳✳✳

As we trooped out to Dad's car to head to the Ladies' Auxiliary luncheon, Mom pulled me aside. "You'll stay close to me, won't you, dear?" she whispered, grabbing my hand. Her own hand was clammy. "It's important to your father that I go to this lunch. I don't want to disappoint him."

"Don't worry, Mom. I'll stay with you," I told her. "You'll be fine. You know all the ladies."

"Thank you, dear," she said, sliding into the back seat beside Jutka.

I sat beside Dad on the front seat. Mom looked smart in a brown tweed suit and matching hat and leather gloves. Jutka was wrapped in her black coat and had a print dress underneath it. I had on my new dress and the navy coat I usually wore to church.

As we drove through the neighborhood, Jutka peered out of the window with interest. Naked trees stood guard on both sides of the road.

"It's a pretty city," she remarked. "So peaceful."

"You'll see more of it tomorrow," Dad said.

Mom cleared her throat. "Jutka, I'd appreciate it if you wouldn't mention anything about . . . um, you know. What I was telling Alexandra."

"You mean you don't want your friends to know who you are, Agi?" Jutka asked quietly.

Mom didn't answer her.

"You don't have to worry about me, Agi. Your secret is safe," Jutka said.

"I won't tell a soul either, Mom," I added.

We all fell silent.

"We're almost there," Dad said finally. "Jutka, are you sure you can't stay with us longer? It's Alexandra's birthday in a couple of weeks. She and her friend Jean always throw a big party. The house is full of young people. It's a very happy time for us."

"There's nothing I'd like better, Jonah, but I can't take more time off from my studies," Jutka said.

"You should start planning your party right away," Mom said to me. "The time is getting close."

"I know, but Jean has been acting weird."

"Did you girls have a fight?"

"Not exactly," I said as Dad maneuvered the car into a parking spot in front of Dr. Wolfe's house. "I don't know what she wants to do. I'll talk to her soon."

The door was opened promptly by Mrs. Wolfe, a tall woman with a kind face. "So nice to see you," she said.

"I brought an old friend with me, Mary," Mom said. "I hope you don't mind. This is Judit Weltner."

Mrs. Wolfe extended a plump hand in Jutka's direction. "How do you do? I'm Mary Wolfe. Welcome to my home."

"Alexandra wanted to come with us too," Mom said with a brittle laugh. "For some reason, she likes the meetings of the Ladies' Auxiliary."

Our hostess glanced in my direction. "The more the merrier," she said.

Mom put her arm through mine as Mrs. Wolfe led us into a living room hazy with cigarette smoke. About two dozen elegantly dressed women were standing in small groups or were perched on the modern Danish furniture. Everybody was chattering and taking sips from sparkling crystal wineglasses. White-coated waiters were passing around tiny canapés.

"Agi, I have to check on something in the kitchen,"

Mrs. Wolfe said. "Would you mind introducing your friend to the ladies?"

As we approached a group of laughing women, Mom's arm tightened in mine. But she swallowed hard and persevered. Only the vein throbbing in her temple showed how nervous she was.

"Hello," she greeted the group. "Nice to see you all again. I'd like you to meet an old friend of mine, Miss Judit Weltner."

Three pairs of eyes stared at us.

"How do you do?" said a fat woman after a moment of awkward silence. She wore a green dress, white gloves, and what looked like a dead bird on her head. "I'm Mrs. Phillips."

Her eyes raked over Jutka. I could see that her scrutiny made Jutka uncomfortable.

"I'm Mrs. Wall," said a blonde woman with a frosty smile. She pointed to the third member of their group. "This is Mrs. Bigelow." Mrs. Bigelow did not deign to change her expression.

To occupy myself, I captured a slice of Velveeta as it floated past on a silver tray.

"It's nice to meet you, ladies," Jutka said with a shy smile.

"Ah, I can hear by your accent that you're a" – Mrs. Wall groped for a word – "newcomer, like Mrs. Gal."

I could sense Jutka tensing up. Mom stepped even closer to me.

Mrs. Wall took a pack of cigarettes and a match from her purse and offered them to her friends and then to Mom and Jutka. They both lit cigarettes and inhaled deeply. Mrs. Bigelow, who was also smoking, picked up a cut-crystal ashtray from the table.

"This is an ashtray," she said to Jutka, pronouncing her words carefully, as if she were speaking to a backward child. "You have to put your ashes in it. Ashes go there, not floor." She gestured to the ashtray and the floor, as if to reinforce her point.

Jutka blushed a fiery red and stubbed out her cigarette in the ashtray that Mrs. Bigelow was holding in front of her nose.

"How –" she began.

"Jutka, don't!" Mom whispered.

The color ran out of Jutka's face. She was so pale that I was afraid she would faint.

She took a deep breath and then, in a dignified voice, said, "Excuse me. I must go and talk to somebody."

I was hot on her heels, dragging Mom behind me. Neither of the other two women followed us or called after us to apologize. We caught up with Jutka by the teak dining-room table. It was overflowing with tiny cucumber sandwiches and glasses of Coke. When Jutka tried to pick up a plate, her hands shook so violently that she dropped it back onto the table with a loud clatter. I flung my arm around her shoulders. I was so angry at those women that I wanted to throttle them.

"I'm so sorry," Mom said.

"Ignore those stupid women!"

"How dare they?" said Jutka. "Who do they think they are? Who do they think *I* am? Agi, to deny who you are for the sake of . . ." she sputtered. "And not to defend yourself!" She bit her lip and stopped talking.

"You don't understand," Mom countered.

"No, I don't understand! You're not being fair to your daughter." She smoothed her hair back into place and seemed to calm down. "But this isn't the time or the place to discuss this."

Mom nodded gratefully.

I piled half a dozen party sandwiches on her plate, and we sat down in a corner of the living room, away from the rest of the group. Jutka and Mom talked about her childhood in Hungary before the war. Their quiet voices brought to life the joys and sorrows of two young girls, decades ago, in a small country on the other side of the ocean.

"Did you enjoy yourself at Agi's meeting, Jutka?" Dad asked at the dinner table that night.

Jutka cut a final mouthful from the sweet cottage-cheese crepe on her plate before replying. "It was interesting," she finally said. "They're very fashionable ladies."

Neither of the two women mentioned the rudeness of the women at the party, so I kept my mouth shut as well. Dad looked a little confused, but he didn't pursue things.

"I don't understand why you haven't planned your birthday party yet," he said, turning to me.

"I have to talk to Jean first."

"Well, what are you waiting for?"

"Nothing." I shrugged. "Jean's been acting so funny lately. I'm not sure she wants to have a party with me."

"Did she say that?" Dad asked.

I shook my head.

"Ask her," he said. "Then at least you'll know where you stand."

"I don't care. . . . Maybe I'm too old for birthday parties."

"*I* am *not* too old," Dad said. "People celebrate their birthdays all through their lives."

"I hope you can work out your problem with Jean," Mom said. "The two of you always had such a good time. What did you fight about?"

"Why do you keep going on about it? It's my birthday and my business!"

"Don't use that tone with your mother!" Dad said.

"If I decide not to have a party, you can't make me have one," I said, jumping up from my seat. "I'm going upstairs!"

"Sit down!" Dad barked. He shook his head. "Nobody will force you to have a party, Alexandra. We just don't understand why you don't want one – if not with Jean, then by yourself."

When I didn't answer him, Jutka broke the tense silence.

"Your crepes are wonderful, Agi," she said. "Just like the crepes your grandmama used to make."

"Do you remember how we used to exchange recipes in the camp?" Mom asked.

"How could I forget?" Jutka said solemnly.

"I got this recipe in Auschwitz," Mom explained to me. "We were so hungry all the time, but we never stopped talking about food."

Dad put his cutlery down. "The pancakes are terrific, but I am so stuffed I can't eat another mouthful," he said, patting his stomach.

"So am I," said Jutka.

When we had cleared the table and washed the dishes, Mom turned to me and said, "Your father only wants what's best for you, dear. If you're not going to have a party with Jean, you should have one by yourself."

I shrugged my shoulders. "I don't know if I want one."

She sighed. "Well, promise me that you'll at least think about it."

"Okay, I promise."

I knew she wouldn't leave me alone until I agreed.

Chapter 15

✳✳✳✳✳✳✳✳✳✳✳✳✳✳✳✳✳✳✳✳✳✳✳✳✳✳✳✳✳✳

My parents let me stay home from school to say goodbye to Jutka. We drove her around and showed her the sights. The car was filled with chatter as she and Mom talked about their days in the old country.

After lunch, it was time for Jutka to leave. With many tearful farewells and promises to write, we drove her to the railroad station downtown. I ran along the platform waving to her as the train pulled out.

By the time we got home, it was too late for me to go to school, so I spent the next two hours half-heartedly tidying the drawers of the dresser in my bedroom. When I realized that I'd lost myself for several minutes staring at the ballerina dancing in my jewel box, I gave up trying to keep busy and sat down on the edge of my bed to think over everything Mom had told me. I tried to guess how my friends would react if I told them my news. Would they still want to be friends with me? I was pretty sure that Molly wouldn't think it was a big deal. But Jean? Would she want to share her birthday with me if she found out that my family was Jewish? I missed talking to her so much, and I so wanted us to be friends again, but I couldn't forget her attitude toward Jacob. Did she dislike Jacob, I wondered, because he was Jewish? It didn't make any sense.

For the first time, it entered my mind that Jacob was having trouble making friends at school because he was Jewish. What would happen to me if I revealed our family's secret? Would the kids in my class still like me? Nobody was beating down Jacob's door with offers of friendship, that much was clear.

I realized that Jacob was the one person who would be pleased to hear my news. I checked my watch. He would be home from school by now. I ran down the stairs to the phone and was already dialing his number before I remembered my promise to Mom. As soon as the receiver was back on the cradle, however, the phone rang. It was Jacob.

"I was just going to call you," I told him.

"What about?" he asked.

"Just to say hi."

"I have to talk to you." He sounded serious.

"What's the matter?"

"Nothing, but I have to tell you something."

"What?"

"Let's meet at the Salisbury House," he said. "I'll tell you everything there."

"Give me fifteen minutes."

"I'll be waiting for you." And with a click, he was gone.

As I went to my closet to get a jacket, I passed the dresser mirror and caught a glimpse of my reflection. I stopped to tidy my ponytail. I pinched my cheeks and put on the light pink lipstick Mom had finally agreed to let me wear. The pink blouse I had on made my skin look whiter, and the thin gold cross gleamed brightly at my throat. Without thinking about it, I slipped it under my collar before I left the room.

I went into the kitchen to find Mom. She was sitting at the table peeling potatoes.

"I'll be out for a while," I explained. "Jacob wants to talk to me."

"You look nice, but where's your cross? You must wear it all the time!"

I pulled out the gold chain and let the cross nestle on top of my shirt.

"Much better," Mom said as she kissed me goodbye.

As soon as I was out of her sight, I slipped the necklace under my collar once again.

I made my way along the gloomy street, past barren trees. I turned the corner and the red roof of the Salisbury House stood out starkly against the glowering sky. When I entered the restaurant, I was wrapped in its sudden warmth. I stopped in the doorway, listening to the buzz of conversation around me. The entire place was hazy from cigarette smoke, and it took me several moments to spot Jacob in a green booth at the far end of the room. He motioned for me to come over.

As I crossed toward him, I saw Jean and Isabel in a booth to my left. They were talking to a girl with long blonde hair with her back to me. They saw me the same instant that I saw them. I raised my hand and waved. Isabel grinned and waved back, but Jean's hands remained clasped in front of her on the table. She leaned over and said something to the girl across from her. When she turned around, I saw that it was Christie Sutherland.

"Oh hi," Jean mumbled when I stopped beside their booth.

"Hi, Alex. It's nice to see you," said Isabel.

Christie kept quiet.

"I'm here to meet Jacob," I said, pointing in his direction. "Come and sit with us."

"I'd like to, but I have to go home now," Isabel said with a friendly smile.

"I don't think so," Jean said. "I have to discuss something with Christie – something private."

I stared at her, speechless. *Private*? What could she want to keep private from me, her best friend?

"Okay," I said as nonchalantly as I could manage. "Well, we should get together soon to plan our birthday party. Do you want to come over to my house tomorrow?"

Jean shot a glance in Christie's direction before stammering, "We'll see."

"We're running out of time. Our birthday is a few weeks away."

"I've been busy. I'll let you know when I have time."

She sounded like a total stranger.

"Well, I better go," I said. "Jacob is waiting."

"I'll phone you," Isabel said.

Jean said goodbye, but Christie didn't even deign to look up. As I made my way to Jacob's booth, I could hear her and Jean whispering to each other and giggling. I was certain they were talking about me.

My feelings were so hurt that I had to swallow hard to prevent myself from crying. It was a relief to reach

Jacob's booth. As soon as I slid into the vinyl seat, he took my hand under the table.

"Your friend Jean doesn't like me," he said, nodding in the direction of the booth where the girls were sitting. "I waved to her when I got here, but she didn't wave back."

"Maybe she didn't see you."

"She saw me," he said. "I can't say I was surprised. I told you before that the kids around here are less friendly than the kids at my old school in Toronto."

"Not all of them."

We were interrupted by a white-aproned waitress. On her bosom was a fancy handkerchief with a badge announcing that her name was Ethel.

"Have you decided yet, or do you need a few more minutes?" she asked.

"I only want a Coke, please."

"You should have something to eat, Alex," Jacob said. "It's my treat today."

We agreed to share an order of french fries, and the woman left.

"You said you wanted to talk to me. Is something wrong? You sounded upset when you called," I said.

He let go of my fingers. I noticed that the cuticles around his nails had been picked raw. He cracked his knuckles and relaxed against the back of the booth. "I'm going to tell you something, Alex, because I want to be honest with you," he said.

"Is it something terrible? Do you want to break up with me?"

"Don't be silly! Of course I don't want to break up with you. I like you too much for that."

"So what's wrong, then?"

"It's my parents – especially my mom . . ." He stopped speaking and began to trace the pattern on the vinyl tablecloth with the fingernail of his right thumb.

"Yes, your parents?" I prompted.

"Well –" He stopped abruptly. A red blush started at the base of his throat and quickly worked its way up to his cheeks.

"Come on, tell me! You're scaring me!" I gave him my most reassuring smile.

"Okay. There's no easy way." He took hold of my hand again and squeezed it tight.

"Tell me," I urged.

He leaned forward, as close to me as he could, and his words came out in a rush. "My folks feel that we're too young to be seeing so much of each other. They think I should date other girls too."

"I thought your family liked me."

"They do. It's only that they – I mean, especially my mom – don't want me to get serious about a girl who isn't . . ." His voice trailed off. He was staring at the tablecloth as if it was the most interesting thing he had ever seen.

"Isn't *what*?" I couldn't keep the impatience out of my voice.

The waitress reappeared just then with two bottles of Coke and a steaming plate of fries that she put in the center of the table.

"Can I bring you something else?" she asked.

Jacob waved her away.

"Please tell me. What's going on?" I pleaded.

"Don't be upset, Alex. It's not your fault. It's just that my parents don't want me to be serious about a girl who isn't Jewish."

I couldn't believe what I was hearing.

"Don't your parents have a problem with my religion too?" he asked. "After all, you never invite me to your house. I haven't even met your mom and dad. My mother says it must be because they don't approve of your going out with a Jew. Is she right?"

My mouth was full of words demanding to be heard, but I held them back when Mom's frightened face swam before my eyes. A promise was a promise, I told myself, even if it involved Jacob. I took a french fry with my free hand and began to nibble on it to gain time.

"I guess your silence tells me all I need to know," Jacob said.

"Don't be silly!" I said. "You're wrong. You're welcome at my house any time."

"Really?"

"Really."

We grinned at each other for a long moment, and then he took hold of my other hand too. "I told my parents that I don't care what your religion is. That I don't want to date anybody else. That I like you a lot, and they'll just have to get used to the idea of our going out."

"I like you a lot too," I said to the top button of his shirt. I forced myself to raise my eyes. "But now," I continued in a stern voice, "let go of my hands!"

He dropped my fingers with a startled look on his face. "Why?" he asked.

"Because our food is getting cold. I like french fries almost as much as I like you."

Chapter 16

I was so upset by everything that had happened in the past few days that I tossed and turned most of the night, wondering who I was. By morning, I'd made a decision.

When I went downstairs, Mom was at the stove and Dad was sitting at the kitchen table, absorbed in his breakfast and the newspaper at the same time.

"Good morning," Mom said. "Breakfast is ready." She took a look at my pale face. "Is everything all right? Are you feeling okay?"

"I'm just tired. I didn't sleep well."

"Neither did I. I was up all night thinking about Jutka. I miss her so much already." She looked at the clock on the wall. "Aren't you running a little late?"

"I'll give you a lift," Dad muttered from behind his newspaper.

"Thanks. But first, I have something to tell both of you."

Dad's newspaper was finally lowered, and Mom sat down on the chair beside mine. Best to get it over with as soon as possible, I thought to myself.

"I did a lot of thinking last night," I began. "I've decided to phone Father Mike and make an appointment to see him after school today. I have some questions for him. I'm also going to tell Jacob the truth. I'm sick of lying to him."

"You mustn't," Mom cried. "No one must know!"

"I can trust both Jacob and Father Mike. They won't tell anybody else if I ask them not to," I said.

"Be reasonable, Agi," Dad said. "I think Alexandra knows what she's doing."

Mom covered her face with her hands. "All right," she finally whispered. "You win. But you must not tell another person. I'd feel much safer if no one knew at all."

"Come in," called Father Mike when I knocked on the door of his study. He waved me to a leather armchair by his desk. I glanced around curiously, since this was the first time I'd ever visited his office. We were surrounded on three sides by shelves groaning under the weight of large books. The priest sat behind an old desk piled high with more books and papers. Above the desk was the familiar sight of Jesus on the cross.

"Nice to see you," he greeted me. "Is everything all right? You sounded worried when you called me." He smiled reassuringly. "If it's your confirmation you're worried about, don't be. I'm certain your parents and I will work something out."

I clasped my hands together tightly. "There won't be a confirmation, Father," I said. Then I told him everything that had happened, starting with my discovery of the old photos in Mom's dresser. When I finished speaking, the priest just looked at me, amazement and pity at war on his face.

"Your poor parents!" he finally said. "Do they know you came to see me?"

"It was Dad who suggested it. At first Mom was reluctant, but she agreed in the end."

"Well, you must all know that your secret is safe with me. I'm bound by rules of confidentiality, and by my own conscience as well, of course."

"Yes, Father."

"So tell me, Alexandra, how do you feel about all of this?"

"I don't know, Father. I'm so confused. I don't know what to think, what to do. If Mom and Dad are Jewish, then I must be too, but I've always thought I was a Catholic. I *feel* like a Catholic."

"Alexandra, you know I'm always ready to instruct you in the ways of the church," he said. He shook his head. "Your poor parents," he repeated. "What terrible suffering they must have endured! And now, to feel that they must deny their past . . ." His face was full of sorrow.

I waited a minute before I spoke again. I didn't want him to think I was being disrespectful, but I needed to voice some of my frustration. "I can't understand how they can pretend to be something they're not," I blurted. "It seems so cowardly!" I was surprised to feel tears running down my face. I brushed them away impatiently with my fists.

Father Mike leaned across his desk, his face just inches from mine. He was so close to me that I could even see the minute wrinkles in his starched white collar.

"Cowardly?" he repeated. "Never, ever do them the injustice of thinking that of them! They sacrificed their past for your sake. They cut themselves off from everything they've known for the love of you! To protect you!"

I spoke slowly, hoping to make myself clear. "I know that Mom and Dad suffered in Europe, Father Mike, but they should realize that nobody in Canada cares about your religion," I said. "Well, most of them don't," I corrected myself. "Anyway, my real concern is what I should do now. What should I tell people? What will my friends say when they find out that we're Jewish? I don't even know how a Jewish person is supposed to feel. Who am I, Father?" My voice came out in a big wail.

"I can't tell you what to do, Alexandra. Only you can decide who you want to tell your secret to, or even if you want to tell it at all. Only you can decide how you want to live your life. I would strongly recommend, however, that you find out more about your family's heritage. Your people died for it, and you owe it to them to learn more. But whatever you decide, I will always be here to answer your questions about the church. The church is always here for you." His expression softened. "I know this can't be easy for you. How old are you? Fourteen? Fifteen?"

"Fourteen next month, Father."

"Old enough to act as a responsible adult, but young enough to be fragile," he said with a smile. "I would advise you to speak to a rabbi. Rabbi David Goltzman of the Herzlia Synagogue is a friend of mine. Do you want to see him? I can call him on your behalf and explain the situation."

I shook my head. "Not yet, Father. I'm not sure what I want to do. I need a little more time." I stood up and headed for the door. "I won't be coming to Sunday school for a while, Father. I want to sort things out first."

"Perhaps that's wise," he said. "I'll explain everything to Sister Ursula."

"Thank you," I said, closing the door softly behind me.

"What do you mean you're Jewish?"

"Shh! Lower your voice, Jacob. People will hear you." I looked around the restaurant. We were sitting in our usual booth at the back of the Salisbury House. Nobody was paying any attention to us. "Haven't you been listening?"

"I have, but I don't get it."

"I didn't believe it either, but it's true. I'm Jewish! Aren't you glad?"

He shrugged his shoulders. "I guess. It doesn't really make a difference to me, but my mother will be happy."

"Oh, you can't tell your parents. I had enough trouble convincing Mom to agree to my telling you. She doesn't want anyone else to know."

Jacob shook his head, a puzzled expression on his face. "Why not?"

I told him about Mom and Dad's experience in the camps, and about what happened to them in Toronto. His expression grew solemn.

"I can see why your mother would feel the way she does. My father lost all of his cousins in the camps. No one talks about it, but lots of people hate Jews, even here.

Do you remember that awful woman at the garage sale?"

I nodded. "How could I forget? Let's not talk about her. It's too depressing."

He frowned. "I wonder if my mother was right and I should have gone to the Jewish school in the North End. There were lots of Jewish kids in my school in Toronto, but I'm the only one here. It might have been easier for me to make friends in a Jewish school."

"You'll make friends at Lord Selkirk. It just takes time."

My words sounded hollow even in my own ears. I knew that I hadn't been invited to Christie's party because I was going out with him, and that that was probably the reason behind Jean's snub the last time we were at the Salisbury House. What would happen when my friends found out that I, too, was Jewish? Perhaps I should never tell anybody else, I said to myself. Maybe I should just forget about being Jewish. But then I remembered that Father Mike had said I owed it to my family to explore my roots. So in spite of my fears, I reached across the table and squeezed Jacob's fingers.

"Don't worry. You'll make friends. In the meantime, you've got me, and I need your help." I smiled my most reassuring smile. "How can I find out what it's like to be Jewish?"

"It sounds like you found out quite a bit from your parents."

"But that was another time, in another world. I need to know what it's like here and now. You're my only Jewish friend. Please help me!"

"Well, the first step is for you to come to synagogue with me on Saturday. Let's meet in front of the Herzlia at ten o'clock." He stood up and began to pull on his jacket.

"I have a better idea. Come and pick me up at home. I'll be ready by nine."

He paused with his hands in mid-air. "You're inviting me to your house, Alex? *Mazel tov!*"

"What's that supposed to mean?"

"It's Hebrew for 'congratulations.' Let it be one of your first lessons in Judaism."

"Thanks!" I said, laughing. "I'm excited to have you meet Mom and Dad."

He nodded. "I've been wanting to see where you live. Afterward, we can walk to synagogue. The Herzlia is ten minutes from your place," he said.

"How should I dress?"

"Same as for church, I guess. The same rules apply."

"He's such a nice boy." Mom patted my arm as she handed me my jacket.

Jacob had spent the last hour making polite conversation with my folks. Mom's frozen expression gradually thawed, and she began speaking normally. Dad was grinning from ear to ear.

"I like your parents," Jacob said as we picked our way through the fresh snow covering the sidewalk.

"I like your family too," I said.

I was glad of the scarf I had wrapped around my throat. It was so cold that our breath formed ghostly spirits in the air. Only six more weeks until Christmas, I said to myself, and then I realized that Christmas would be very different that year.

"I told my parents I was taking you to synagogue with me," Jacob said. "They wanted to know why, so I told them you were interested in the service. Come for lunch at our house when it's over."

"Thanks. I'd love to."

We turned the corner of the street.

"We're almost there," Jacob said, grasping my elbow to prevent me from falling on a patch of ice.

The synagogue was a gray stucco building with a flat roof. Only the enormous stained-glass windows reminded me of St. Stephen's. We joined a group of people climbing the stairs.

"Careful! The steps are slippery," Jacob warned as he took my hand.

We hung our coats in a cloakroom, and then Jacob slapped a yarmulke on the back of his head and wrapped his shoulders in a white shawl with a pattern of black lines and fringes at both ends. I fingered the fringe.

"You like my tallis?" he asked.

"It's beautiful."

"My parents gave it to me for my bar mitzvah," he said. "Let's go inside."

We entered a large sanctuary filled with wooden pews. I slid into the last row, and Jacob sat down beside me. I looked around. It was a plain room, without any pictures or statues on the walls. Light filtered through the stained glass and fell upon a small podium at the front of the room. Four men were gathered around a small table covered with a royal blue velvet cloth. One of them, middle-aged with a grizzled beard, was reading from a book and chanting loudly in a foreign language.

"That's Rabbi Goltzman," Jacob whispered. "He's a good guy."

Behind the podium, on the east wall, was a tall cabinet covered by blue velvet curtains embroidered in gold. A lamp dangled from the ceiling in front of the cabinet. It was lit despite the brightness of the room.

I looked around curiously. The pews were filled with people of all ages, and there were a few little kids running around. The men wore prayer shawls and their heads were covered by yarmulkes like Jacob's. The women were elegantly dressed in suits, hats, and gloves. I didn't recognize a single soul until my eyes fell upon old Mrs. Steinberg, who lived across the street from us. I sank down in my seat, hoping that she wouldn't see me. Suddenly, she screwed her head around and her mouth parted in a surprised O. She leaned close to her neighbor and started whispering behind an open palm. Then her companion turned around and stared at me. I was certain they were talking about me.

Everybody was chatting with their neighbors. Nobody seemed to be paying much attention to the people at the podium. It was so different from the total silence expected of us at St. Stephen's. If any of us even whispered out of turn, Sister Ursula's eagle eye promised future punishment.

A red-headed boy whose face was covered with freckles slipped into the pew beside us.

"Hi," he whispered.

"You're late. The rabbi is going to kill you!" Jacob said. "Rabbi Goltzman is our teacher at religious school," he explained to me. "He expects us to come early for services. Alex," he added, "I want you to meet Shane. He's on my bowling team."

"Luckily for you," the boy said, slapping Jacob on the back. "Jake told me that you'd be coming to synagogue. Do you like it?"

"I don't know. It's different from what I expected. Is it always so noisy?"

"Always!" He looked around the sanctuary. "Where are your parents?" he asked Jacob.

"They'll be here soon. Marnie too."

"Does Marnie go to religious school as well?" I asked.

"She'll be starting next year." He groaned. "I'm sure that Mom will expect me to take care of her." His face brightened and he said, "Why don't you come with me? The classes are interesting, and Rabbi Goltzman is a good teacher."

I shrugged my shoulders. "I don't know . . ."

"Well, think about it," he said. He took a prayer book from a shelf attached to the back of the pew in front of us. "I'd better pay attention. Rabbi Goltzman gets mad if we goof off."

He handed me another prayer book and opened it for me near the back. It was filled with letters I couldn't read.

"It's written in Hebrew," he explained. "We read the prayer book back to front, and each line from right to left."

"Hello, Jacob, Alexandra," somebody behind us said in a frosty voice. It was Mrs. Pearlman. Jacob's family had arrived. They sat down beside us.

"You're late," Jacob said.

"Marnie had trouble getting up," Mr. Pearlman said.

The girl gave him an angry look, but before she could answer, the entire congregation stood up. I stood up with them. Everybody around us began to sing. One of the men at the podium pulled aside the drapes of the cabinet and swung open its doors to reveal several velvet-covered cylindrical objects decorated with beautiful silver crowns and silver shields. The rabbi took one of the large cylinders out of the cabinet.

"He's taking out the Torah," Jacob whispered. "They'll be reading from it."

I let the words of the compelling hymn wash over me. They made me feel as if I had just woken up from a deep slumber and was swimming in an emerald sea full of possibilities. The music embraced me, soaking into every pore of my being until I was lost in an ocean of waves, each different and unique but all coming together as one. The sea of music was strange and comforting at the same time. I felt at peace, as if I was a traveler who had just returned from a long voyage to a home she hardly recognized. My heart was filled with longing and confusion.

I was startled when Jacob tapped me on the shoulder. The two-hour service had passed in a haze.

"It's over," he said as he folded his prayer shawl. "Let's go. I'm hungry." He turned to Shane. "You come too," he said.

"Thanks, but I can't. My mom is expecting me."

Jacob's parents were already on their way out the door, leaving without saying goodbye. Only Marnie turned back to us, waving before her mother yanked on her arm to hurry her up.

"Do you mind if I take a raincheck?" I said to Jacob. "It was a lot to take in for the first time. I want to go home and think about everything I saw."

"I wish you'd come, but I understand," he said. "How about coming to see me bowl next week, on Sunday afternoon? It's my BBYO team's final game. We have a good chance for the cup."

"I wouldn't miss it for anything. Where shall I meet you?"

"I'll pick you up at two. We're bowling at Grosvenor Lanes. We can take the bus. It stops right in front."

Chapter 17

Jacob arrived half an hour early. His face was flushed and he seemed excited as he greeted us.

"So, Jacob, Alexandra tells us that today is your big game," Mom said. "Are you nervous?"

"I just don't want to let my team down," Jacob said. "If we win, we'll be awarded the trophy for our division."

"I'm sure you'll do your best," Dad said.

"I have to talk to you," Jacob mouthed behind my parents' backs.

"I'd like Jacob to help me with a math problem," I announced. "Let's go down to the rec room. I left my school bag down there." For Mom and Dad's benefit, I added, "We only have a few minutes before we have to leave."

I turned on the lights at the bottom of the stairs. Jacob sprawled on one of the orange beanbag chairs, and I perched on the edge of the couch. He looked rather pleased with himself but didn't say a word.

I broke the silence. "So what did you want to tell me?"

He reached into his pocket and took out a small package wrapped in shiny blue paper. He put it into my hand and wrapped my fingers around it. "I bought you a present," he said.

I was so surprised that I couldn't find the right words. "It's so nice of you," I finally stammered, tearing off the wrapping to reveal a black velvet box. Inside glimmered a delicate silver chain with a small six-pointed star hanging from it. "It's beautiful! Thank you." I hugged and kissed him.

"It's a Star of David – a Jewish star," he said. "Let me put it on you."

I lifted my ponytail and he fastened the chain around my neck. I walked up to the mirror behind the wet bar in the corner of the room to admire myself. The star glistened brightly against my pink mohair sweater.

"I'd better hide it away for now," I told him.

He nodded. "Good idea. You don't want everybody wondering why you have a Magen David."

I traced the sharp outline of the star with my fingers, then slipped it below the collar of my sweater. It clinked against the gold cross that was already resting at the base of my throat.

Jacob stood up. "We have to get going or we'll be late," he said.

The bus stopped right in front of Grosvenor Lanes. Groups of chattering kids of all ages were streaming into the building. "Welcome to Our 15th Annual Roll-Off!" proclaimed a large banner on one wall of the spacious lobby. A lunch counter was attached to an adjacent wall. All the stools in front of it were occupied by hungry bowlers wolfing down hot dogs and guzzling bottles of Coca-Cola.

"We're playing against a team from St. Mark's Tech," Jacob said. "Let's see which alley we've drawn."

We walked up to a large board in the corner of the hall. Jacob ran his finger down the side of the schedule.

"Here we are. Lane one is ours."

Wide double doors led us into the bowling alley. Jacob had his own bowling shoes, but I had to rent a pair for a nickel. His team was waiting for him by lane one. I was glad to see Shane's friendly face.

"Why are you so late?" he asked. "We were worried that you wouldn't get here on time." While he talked to Jacob, the rest of their teammates were staring at me.

"I stopped off at Alex's place first," Jacob said.

"It'll be nice to have a cheerleader around," said a short boy with heavy-duty acne and an infectious smile. Like his teammates, he was wearing a light blue sweater with a white Star of David on the back and the words "B'Nai B'rith Tigers" above it.

Jacob took an identical sweater out of his gym bag and pulled it over his shirt. I sat down on a bench next to a rack of five-pin bowling balls while he introduced me to the rest of the boys – Sam, the one with the infectious smile; a tall, pale boy called David; and a fat, short one whose name was Adam.

"Did you hear anything about those gorillas?" asked Jacob, nodding his head in the direction of the neighboring lane.

The five boys gathering there were much taller and heavier than Jacob and his friends. They wore orange T-shirts that declared them to be the St. Mark's Tech Strikers.

"They seem older than us," said Shane, "but they must be in grade nine, like we are, or they wouldn't be in our division."

"St. Mark's is a technical school for problem kids who flunked out of regular school," Adam said. "They've probably all repeated a grade."

"I heard that they're great bowlers, especially the guy with the ducktail," said Sam, pointing to a tall, heavy-set blond boy with a pockmarked face. "His name is Steve Robinson. He'll be bowling against you, Jacob."

The pinsetters appeared on their ledges, and a whistle blew.

"Time to get to work," Jacob said.

Shane was our lead-off. It was immediately obvious that he was outranked by the pimply-faced Striker bowling next to him. At the end of the game, Jacob and Steve Robinson, the anchors, faced off. Jacob's near-perfect game was matched by Robinson's, and St. Mark's led with 1210 pins to our 1190. The Strikers howled and thumped one another on the back.

"You'd think they'd already won," Jacob complained. "But we've got four more games to play. Let's show them what we're made of!"

In the second game, we beat the Strikers 1190 to 1180. Game three was a draw, with 1230 points earned by each team. By the fourth game, I could see that the Tigers were getting nervous. While we waited for the pinsetters to clean up the deadwood, Jacob leaned over to Shane and said: "Go get 'em!"

Shane's face was shiny with sweat. He took three long steps forward and threw a beautiful hook, knocking down all the pins except the head pin. The Strikers' lead-off answered with two strikes in a row. By the end of the game, we were down a total of fifty-seven pins.

"It looks hopeless," muttered Sam as we waited for the pinboy to reset the pins. "They're better than us."

"We're as good as they are!" Jacob replied fiercely.

Sam stood up. "I'll do my best not to let you down, guys," he said, squaring his shoulders.

But his best wasn't good enough. By the time Jacob stood up for the last frame of the final game, we were still trailing the Strikers by eight pins.

"Good luck," I called to him.

Jacob's face was calm, but I could see his shirt moving in rhythm to his pounding heart. He took five short steps forward, spreading his fingers around the ball as he lifted it to chest level and rotated it. His arm went back, then forward, and the ball thundered down the lane, knocking down all of the pins in its path.

"Strike! Strike!" The Tigers jumped up and down with joy.

I stomped my feet and called out, "Hooray! Hooray!"

Jacob did not seem to hear us. He was staring ahead with narrowed eyes, his concentration unbroken. He was intent on bowling a perfect frame. Two more strikes followed.

"We're leading by thirty-seven pins," cried David. "We've got them!"

For the first time, I saw doubt creep into Jacob's eyes. "They can still easily beat our score," he said.

"They won't," said Adam.

Jacob hushed him as Steve Robinson took four steps forward and threw a beautiful hook shot. All the pins tumbled before it. His next ball was also a strike.

"We're finished," Shane said glumly.

Jacob was silent, waiting for the last ball to be thrown. Even I had to admire Steve's form – perfect concentration, a beautiful delivery. His ball hurtled down the lane, and then we all heard the sickening crack of a punched head pin that left four others standing. Our team erupted in howls of joy. Steve was rigid, staring at the standing pins in disbelief. Then he began to curse, using words I did not even know existed. He turned toward us with an angry glare and stepped over into our lane. We all fell silent.

"Good game, man," Jacob said to him, sticking out his hand.

The bigger boy pushed his hand aside and spat on Jacob's shoes. "Kike!" he cried. "You were lucky. That's why you won."

Before I even knew what was happening, Jacob had jumped on Steve and knocked him to his knees. Then all of the boys in both alleys joined the fray. Within minutes, the Tigers were being devoured by the Strikers. Jacob was flat on his back with Steve on his chest, knocking his head into the gutter.

"You don't look much like a winner to me now, Jew boy!" Steve snarled.

"Take it back!" Jacob repeated between merciless punches to his head.

Suddenly, Olga's face swam in front of my eyes. Her lips were twisted into a sneer of hate. "I don't work for kikes," she hissed. Without giving myself the opportunity to think, I jumped on Steve's back, my arms around his shoulders, my fists beating on his chest. "How dare you call Jacob names! How dare you, you creep!" I sputtered. As he tried to shake me off, Jacob rolled out from underneath him and began to pull himself up.

Just then, the manager of Grosvenor Lanes and his assistant appeared. They pried me off Steve and dropped me to the floor with a loud thud.

"Stop it! Stop it!" they yelled as they separated the fighting boys.

"He started it," Steve said sullenly, pointing his finger at Jacob. By now, a crowd had gathered around us.

"He provoked me," Jacob muttered.

"Nothing excuses such behavior," the manager said, his face full of disgust. "I'm surprised at you, Pearlman. I thought you were a good kid."

I pulled on the manager's sleeve. "He insulted Jacob!" I said, pointing at Steve. "Jacob had no choice. He had to defend himself."

The manager shook his head. "I don't care who's wrong and who's right. Nothing excuses violence like that, and no trophy will be presented this year. I want you all out of here immediately!"

He stormed off before we could protest, his assistant following in his wake. With a final snicker in our direction, Steve and his cronies left. The crowd around us also dispersed.

"Well, I guess it's time to go," Shane said, shrugging his shoulders.

"I'm sorry, guys," said Jacob. "I shouldn't have lost my temper. It cost us the trophy."

"I'd have done the same," Sam said.

"So would I," said David.

"Me too," added Adam.

The house was empty when I got home. Dad must have talked Mom into going for a drive. I went up to my room and lay down on my bed. I realized that I knew how Jacob felt. Steve's insults had made me afraid and powerless, just like Jacob. His insults had become personal. For the first time, I began to understand why Mom wanted to pretend to be somebody she was not. I also began to understand that I had to face the hatred.

While I was brushing my teeth before bed, Dad called up the stairs that somebody wanted to talk to me on the phone. I threw on my robe, pulled on my slippers, and padded downstairs.

"I hope your parents aren't mad at me for calling you so late," said Jacob.

I looked at Dad's annoyed face. "Of course not. What's up?"

"First of all, I want to thank you for helping me this afternoon. I never knew you were so strong." He laughed.

"You'd better be careful how you behave with me," I joked back.

His voice became serious. "When I told my parents what happened at the bowling alley, they were furious. They grounded me for fighting, but then Dad drove me back to speak to the manager. As soon as he understood exactly what had happened, he decided to award us the trophy after all."

"That's terrific! Congratulations!"

"Thanks." He sighed. "The manager wanted to make Steve apologize to me, but I told him not to bother. He wouldn't mean it," he said. "I just called the other guys on the team. I thought you'd want to know too."

"I'm glad you phoned."

"The team is happy about the cup, but what happened this afternoon ruined it for me."

"Don't be silly! It wasn't your fault."

"I should have controlled my temper. That's the best way to handle such an ignoramus. The world is full of them, and hitting them won't solve anything."

"Sometimes it doesn't hurt," I said, remembering Steve's shocked expression as Jacob knocked him to his knees. "Anyway, it's good you were given the trophy. You deserved it."

"Thanks," he said flatly. "Well, I'd better let you go now," he added. "Time for bed."

I never heard him mention the trophy again.

At school the next morning, Molly asked me if I wanted to go with her to the school library to find some books for our English assignment. I said I had no time, but it was as if a lightbulb had gone on in my head. I called Mom from the payphone in the lunchroom at noon and told her I had to go and do some research after school.

Luckily, I had a couple of tickets in my pocket, so I could take the bus to the main branch of the public library, on William Avenue. Since it was the biggest library in the city, I knew it would have more of the books I needed.

I just loved the library – from the musty scent that assailed my nostrils as I pushed open the imposing double doors to the sight of the thousands of volumes lined up on their dark wood shelves. This day, I went straight to the stern librarian, who was seated behind a large oak desk. My footsteps sounded like thunder in the silence of the room.

"Can I help you?" she whispered.

"I want to find out what happened to the Jewish people in Europe during the war," I said. I'd never noticed that my voice could boom.

She stared at me coldly through her pince-nez. "Why?" she finally asked. "That's not a suitable topic for a young girl."

I stood there, frozen. It had never entered my mind that I would have to justify my choice of books. "We have to write an essay about it for social studies class," I eventually said.

She shook her head disapprovingly. "Well," she said, "if you insist, I'll show you some materials in our reference department. You're welcome to look at the books one at a time, but you cannot take them out."

I followed her to the back of the library and several glass-fronted cabinets full of heavy volumes. She unlocked the door of one and pulled out a very large book bound in black paper. *Auschwitz* was its title.

"Start with this one. You can look at it here," she said, pointing to the wooden table and chairs beside the cabinet. "Please return the book to me when you're done. Then I'll give you another one."

She locked the door of the cabinet and was gone.

I took a pencil and a notebook from my school bag and laid them carefully on the table, ready to take notes. I decided to leaf through the book before beginning to read it. It was full of black-and-white photographs. At first, I couldn't process them. Skeletal figures in striped pajamas. Barbed wire and buildings with high chimneys belching dark smoke into the air. Mountains of bodies. The pictures were relentless. I began to weep silently, mourning the loss of the grandparents, aunts, uncles, and cousins I was never to know. Then I cried for Mom and Dad, for all they had suffered, for the humiliation they had endured. I cried for their past, with its painful memories, and for their future, which was forever changed.

I must have made more noise than I realized, for suddenly there was a tap on my shoulder and the book was whisked out of my hands.

"I knew it was a bad idea to let you read this," the librarian said kindly. "Which school did you say you go to? I have a good mind to call your teacher and let him know what I think of his terrible assignment!"

"Please don't," I muttered, shrugging into my jacket and hustling out the door as quickly as I could manage.

Mom was in the kitchen when I got home. Dad was still in his office, so I was able to run upstairs without being seen. After I'd washed my face, I looked like I always did, although my eyes were slightly red. Only then did I go downstairs to say hello to Mom. I told her that I'd been at the library with Molly. I never told her about the photographs I'd seen.

Chapter 18

✳✳✳✳✳✳✳✳✳✳✳✳✳✳✳✳✳✳✳✳✳✳✳✳✳✳✳✳✳✳✳✳

"Hurry up! Molly and her mother will be here soon," I called up the stairs.

I was sitting in the living room, dressed in my Girl Guide uniform, waiting for Mom to get ready for our tea at the Sports Club. Dad was out on a house call, so Mrs. Windsor was driving us.

When another few minutes passed and there was still no sign of Mom, I bounded up the staircase to find her. She was lying on her bed in her slip, a wet cloth covering her eyes.

"I have a migraine," she said. "I can't go with you. Molly and her mother will take you."

"You promised you'd come!" My voice came out in a childish wail.

"I'm very sorry."

"You went to the Ladies' Auxiliary meeting!" I said.

"I knew all the women there. There will be too many strangers at your tea."

I sat down on the side of her bed and burst into tears. "Please, Mom, you've got to come. All the mothers will be there! I'll stay with you the whole time, I promise. I'll even hold your hand."

She sat up, swung her legs over the side of the bed, and put her arms around my shoulders.

"Stop crying, dear. I know I'm unfair to you." She stared at the floor for a minute, deep in thought, then raised her head and squared her shoulders. "Take my black suit out of the closet while I brush my hair and put on some lipstick."

Ten minutes later, we were in Mrs. Windsor's car. Mom was sitting up front, beside Mrs. Windsor, while Molly and I were in the back seat. On my knees I was balancing a pretty plate with a cherry cheesecake on it, and Molly was clutching a fancy ceramic bowl filled with chocolate chip cookies.

"Why haven't you been coming to church with us, Alexandra?" Molly's mother said in a kind voice. "We miss you."

I was saved from having to respond because just then Mrs. Windsor pulled up in front of the Sports Club and became preoccupied with maneuvering the car into a parking spot by the curb. As we were getting out, Mom grabbed my hand and held on tight.

Mrs. Cowan was waiting to greet us in the spacious lobby. "Put your baking on the buffet table in the banquet room and then circulate among the guests. And don't forget to entertain your mothers," she said to Molly and me. "Remember! You're the hostesses."

The banquet hall looked perfect. Our patrol had spent the previous afternoon spreading white cloths over the large round tables scattered throughout the room. The tables were set with the club's monogrammed china, sparkling crystal glasses, and gleaming silverware, and each plate held a cloth napkin folded in the shape of a fan. We had made gallons of lemonade and stored it in glass pitchers in the club's refrigerators. We'd even festooned the walls with crepe paper and taped up large signs welcoming the members of Girl Guide Company No. 2 and their mothers to the annual tea. I was tired by the time we'd put everything in order, for there were only four of us to do the work. Jean had stayed at home with the flu.

"Doesn't the room look glamorous? It was certainly worth all the effort, and our baking looks yummy," Molly said. "I'll take the lemonade out of the fridge and put a pitcher on each table."

"I'll check off the baking." I had made a list of what each girl was supposed to bring.

"I'll come with you, dear." Mom moved to follow me.

"Hi, Alex," said somebody behind me.

It was Isabel. Jean and Christie were standing next to her, but they both seemed so absorbed in the placards on the walls that they didn't say hello to me. I thought of all the happy times Jean and I had shared, and suddenly I wanted to try to put things right.

"Hi, girls," I said in a friendly tone. "It's nice to see you."

Christie turned and left without answering me.

"What's the matter with her?" Isabel asked.

"Forget about it." I turned to Jean. "I'm glad you're feeling better."

The color rose in her cheeks. "Hi, Alex," she mumbled. "I'm still a bit sick, but I came anyway. Welcome to our tea, Mrs. Gal, Mrs. Windsor."

The words did not come easily, but I felt I had to say them. "I've been wanting to talk to you, Jean. Come over to my house after the tea so we can plan our birthday party."

She blushed again. "I didn't have the chance to tell you before, but my mother thinks I should have my own party this year. I'm sorry."

Molly had rejoined us while we were talking. "But you and Alex have celebrated your birthdays together since kindergarten!"

Mom also opened her mouth to speak, but I squeezed her fingers so tightly that she fell silent.

"Your mother's right, Jean. A separate party would be fun!" I didn't want her to know how disappointed I was.

Isabel stared at us in turn, sensing that something was wrong. "Jean and I made party sandwiches," she finally said.

By now, the banquet hall was filling up with Guides in their uniforms and their mothers in their Sunday best. Even the youngest girls were bringing some kind of baking.

"I think it's time to boil the water for the tea," Isabel said, taking Jean by the arm. "We'll see you later. The Canaries are all sitting together at table nine." She made a sour face. "When I made up the seating plan, Mrs. Cowan asked to be put at our table, so we'll have to be on our best behavior."

A few minutes later, we were gathered around our table, our plates piled high with different kinds of sandwiches and cakes. I stole a glance at Mom. She seemed serene, but she was grasping my hand tightly under the tablecloth.

"You girls are to be congratulated," Mrs. Cowan said.

"You worked hard and did a wonderful job. You earned your hostess badges fair and square."

"It was fun planning everything," Molly said. She was sitting next to me.

"Our girls were adamant about doing everything themselves," said Mrs. Windsor. "Fortunately, they had Mrs. Gal's excellent recipes for guidance." She took a bite of my cheesecake. "This is the best cheesecake I have ever tasted!"

I could see by Mom's smile how much the compliment pleased her.

"Would anybody like coffee?" I asked.

"Thank you," said Jean's mother, holding out her cup.

I took it to the buffet table and filled it with strong, black coffee. As soon as I sat back down, Mom took hold of my hand again.

"Ah! Nothing like a cup of coffee after such delicious pastry," Jean's mother said.

"If you want to taste really good pastry, you must go to Europe," Mrs. Cowan said. "My husband and I spent last summer in Switzerland. He wanted to go hiking in the mountains."

Mom smiled wistfully. "When I was a young girl, before the war, our family used to spend our winter vacations in Lucerne. I still remember how lovely the city was."

"It is, isn't it?" said Mrs. Cowan.

"I bet you can't get better cheesecake than this even in Lucerne," said Mrs. Windsor.

"This is the first time I've been to the Sports Club," Christie said, changing the subject. "This banquet hall is so" – she searched for a word – "elegant."

"It certainly is," Mrs. Cowan said. "There's also a gym, indoor tennis courts, and a swimming pool. Our family spends every weekend here. Many of our friends have also taken out memberships," she continued, between mouthfuls of cheesecake. "Best of all, it's a private club, so none of *them* is able to join."

"A good thing, too," Jean's mother said.

Christie's mother nodded her agreement.

"What do you mean, Mrs. Cowan?" Molly asked. "Who are you talking about?"

Mrs. Cowan leaned forward and whispered in a confidential manner, "Why, Jews, my dear. Who else would I be talking about? Our membership committee has an unwritten rule not to let Jews into the club. Thank goodness none of you is Jewish." She chuckled. "If even one of my Guides was a Jew, we couldn't have held our tea in this beautiful facility."

Mom's grasp tightened so much that she was hurting my hand. Her face was ashen, then it turned a fiery red. As I stared at her, a flood of memories overwhelmed me – Mrs. Cowan's insult to Jacob, the fight in the bowling alley, the photographs I'd seen in the book at the library. I didn't dare contemplate the memories that must have rushed to Mom's mind.

I sat there rigidly, unable to speak, bound by my promise to her. Suddenly, she leaned toward me, pulled her hand out of my grasp, and quietly, with tremendous dignity and determination, said, "Tell them, my dear. Tell them."

I turned to Mrs. Cowan. "I guess Mom and I should leave, then. We are two of 'them.' We are Jewish."

A deathly silence greeted my announcement. Nine pairs of startled eyes focused on me.

I stood up. "Come on, Mom. Let's go. We're not wanted here."

She rose from the table and put her arm around my shoulders. "I'm so proud of you," she said.

Just then, Molly jumped to her feet. "If you're leaving, Alex, I'm going with you!"

"So am I," said her mother, standing up beside her.

Isabel and her mother were next to rise.

"You should be ashamed of yourself," Isabel's mother said to the Guide leader.

"What's the matter with you people?" Mrs. Cowan cried. "Surely you're not taking *their* side?" she asked, pointing her finger at us.

"It's not a question of sides," Mrs. Windsor said. "It's a question of human decency."

Just then, my eyes met Jean's. Her face was contorted with hate.

"I knew something was going on when you started to go out with a dirty Jew," she said. "But it never entered my mind that you were one yourself."

"Shut up, Jean!" Molly snapped. "No one wants to hear your hateful opinions."

As I turned to walk away, I caught one last sight of Christie and Jean, snickering away while Jean's mother stared off into the air, sipping the coffee I had poured for her.

"Why didn't you tell me?" Molly asked on the way home.

"It's a long story. We'll talk later, when there's more time."

"I'm so sorry that you were subjected to that terrible woman," Mrs. Windsor said. "She's not fit to be around young people. I'm calling Guide headquarters tomorrow. They'll be appalled to learn what happened this afternoon." She looked at Molly in the rear-view mirror. "You're not going back to Guides until she's replaced."

"I don't want to," Molly replied.

"Neither do I," I said.

Soon, we pulled up in front of our house, and at last Mom and I were alone.

"They're good people," she said as she put the key into the lock. "I'm so glad Molly is your friend. She's very loyal." She sighed. "I wish I could say the same of Jean. I'm sorry about her. I know how much her friendship meant to you."

I shook my head. "I didn't know what she was really like."

"I was very proud of you this afternoon, Alexandra," she said, patting my cheek. "You're a brave girl."

"Not as brave as you, Mom!" I wiped away the tears that had welled up in my eyes. "Well, I guess Dad won't be playing tennis at the Sports Club any longer."

"Now you can understand why he never took us there. He hated to lie on the application, but he knew their rule. All of his friends play there, and he couldn't really explain why he wouldn't join too."

"I don't blame him, Mom."

"Neither do I. All the same, it's not easy pretending to be somebody you're not. Nobody knows that better than I." She sighed again. "I thought I could spare you all this hurt, darling, but I was wrong. I should have realized that we can never escape our past. It's just part of who we are."

Later that evening, we told Dad everything. The fury in his face frightened me. He slammed his fist into his open palm. "I wish there was something I could do to protect you," he said. "But what can anyone do against such unreasoned hate? Nothing will change the minds of such ignorant people."

"You're right, Jonah," Mom said. "And you were also right about everything else. I was wrong. We cannot make the past disappear. We are who we are as a result of it." She smiled. "I was so afraid that people would find out who we are. Yet now that everything is out in the open, I feel as if a great weight has been lifted from my shoulders."

"So do I," Dad said. "It's hard to live a lie, but there will be a price to pay now that the truth is out."

"What do you mean?" I asked.

"Some of my patients will leave me," he said. "Don't worry. It can't be helped. We'll manage somehow."

"Well, I'm still glad that we don't have to pretend any longer," I said. "I feel free!" I flung my arms into the air. "I've been thinking about something else too," I added. "You were right – I should have a birthday party. I'm not going to let Jean ruin it for me. Molly will help me plan it, and I'll invite Isabel and some other girls from Guides."

"Good girl!" Dad said, beaming at me.

"Can I also invite the boys from Jacob's bowling team?"

Dad chuckled. "Why not?"

"I'll take your new dress to Freddy's tomorrow to be cleaned," Mom said. "It's time I met Jacob's parents." She stood up from her chair. "It's cold outside, but it's so fresh and beautiful. I feel like going for a walk."

Dad stood up. "Good idea! Let's go."

"Jonah, would you mind if I went by myself?" Mom asked. "I have a lot of thinking to do."

Dad and I just stared at her.

As she hobbled out of the room, Dad wiped a tear from the corner of his eye. I pretended not to notice.

Epilogue

****

I looked around my room. The white-and-gold furniture, ruffled pink bedspread, and pink carpet looked so pretty. My eyes fell on my wall and the poster of Elvis in his army uniform. He was as cute as ever.

I walked to my dresser mirror and stared at the face looking back at me. The girl in the mirror looked sad and happy at the same time. I undid the clasp of the cross that was hanging under the collar of my shirt, hiding the silver necklace that Jacob had given me. The cross gleamed golden in my palm. I put it in my jewel box, under my rosary. It would always be special to me. The ballerina was twirling a mournful farewell as I closed the lid.

Next, I pulled out the Star of David and looked at it glistening brightly against my clothes. But I hesitated. I'm not ready, I said to myself. Not yet. And I slipped the necklace back into its hiding place under my collar.

I knew there were two more things that I had to do. First, I went downstairs and called Jacob to tell him that I would go with him to his next Jewish school class.

Finally, I sat down at my desk and took out a clean sheet of loose-leaf paper. I knew exactly what I wanted to write:

Dear Mom and Dad,

Thank you.
I understand.
I love you.

Alexandra

Sometimes it's easier to write what's in your heart than it is to say it.

Glossary

Auschwitz	a concentration camp run by the Nazis in Poland during the Second World War
bar mitzvah	a religious ceremony for Jewish boys when they reach thirteen
confirmation	a ceremony during which a baptized person becomes a full member of the Christian Church
DP camp	temporary shelter for people who have been left homeless or been forced to flee because of war
Magen David	the Jewish Star of David
Mass	a Catholic ceremony commemorating the Last Supper
Shabbos	the Jewish Sabbath, or day of rest and religious observance
tallis	a prayer shawl
Torah	the first five books of the Bible; also called the Pentateuch
yarmulke	a skullcap worn by Jewish men